At The Bottom Of Another World's Ocean . . .

Crouching low, I was hidden in the mass of bubbles released from the outsized neck of the module. So was what emerged. I did not get a clear look until it had passed through the tube and was heading upward toward the swimmer.

In the past hour I had seen an illegal alien and illegal warships. Now I was seeing something else. The rising creature was a Naumum, which, on Usulkan, was supposed to have been one of a kind—and very dead.

What was even more depressing was the next realization which greeted my eyes. The great black beast had not been the only being which had come from the module.

The three dart rifles were trained directly at my gut.

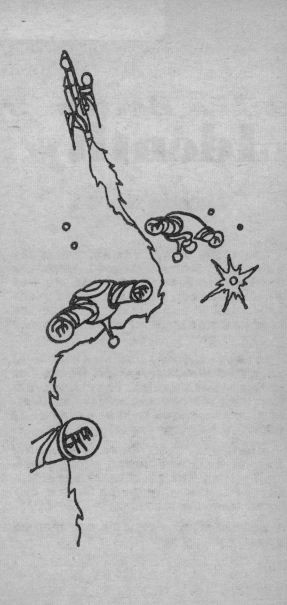

Identity Seven

by
ROBERT LORY

DAW BOOKS, INC.

DONALD A. WOLLHEIM, PUBLISHER

1301 Avenue of the Americas
New York, N. Y.   10019

DEDICATION

This, my latest,
is for Shana Erin,
our latest.

FIRST PRINTING: MARCH 1974

1 2 3 4 5 6 7 8 9

Printed in the U.S.A.

Identity
Seven

CHAPTER 1

How do you mourn someone like Kalian Pendek?

How do you mourn someone who, on the one hand, you know so well—too well—and, on the other, you know not at all?

It was a first for me, a real first. I didn't know how to react, not having had the experience necessary for any kind of conditioned reaction. So maybe my reaction was not what was expected of me. But I didn't give a good damn as to what was expected of me. If the fact that my hands seemed to wring nervously bothered anybody, that was his problem. So was the fact that beads of sweat popped out from the pores of my forehead.

Lack of control? The cool and rational knuckling under to the wild and irrational?

A possible interpretation, but the hell with it. Kalian Pendek didn't have much of a chance to think on such matters.

Kalian Pendek never knew what hit him.

Or who.

Although if he had survived maybe he might have made an educated guess. But he hadn't survived.

I saw the whole thing. Correction. What I saw was:

Kalian Pendek stepping from the rear ramp of the Sub-Oceanic Transport Building to his awaiting chauffeured skimmer which gleamed, as did the tall building itself, in the bright midmorning sunlight common to the planet of Usulkan. Kalian Pendek, early-fortyish-looking. Close-cropped hair, black with streaks of gray, low widow's peak almost reaching down to the almost-meeting black bushy eyebrows. Sharp facial features, handsome in a nonfashionable way, nose and chin perhaps thrust a bit too forward. Reddish bronze skin. Six-three frame, strong build without appearing overmuscled, attired this morning in white satiney trousers and tunic.

Expensive clothes, but not ostentatious. Durable and quiet, although the bright sun brought out the satiney brilliance. As it did the single jewel the man wore over his breast. As it did the black boots flashing in the sunlight as—

Their owner strides across the ramp toward the open panel of the private skimmer which has been pulled wharfside in the special presidential dock. From flashing boots to skimmer there are now a dozen paces, maybe fifteen. For a man of Kalian Pendek's size and long stride, certainly no more than that.

He never made it.

The skimmer normally carried one pilot, two crew. All three were aboard, I could see; all three no doubt looking forward to passing a couple of free hours in the central part of Crown City while the Sub-Oceanic president carried on his business. They enjoyed these trips, I knew. I had taken several such short voyages with them. I recognized Garth, the pilot, and Seraso; the remaining member of the crew was new to me. Not unusual, as the company employed several men for its fleet of topside skimmers, most of them reassigned from the sub-sea carriers due to age or health considerations.

Three on the skimmer, all in sight. Kalian Pendek and another man—his personal aide, Satu—now approaching.

The lithe little yellow Satu handing the president a serpent-hide briefcase.

And then the sudden turning. Kalian Pendek turning his head—looking, it seemed, right into my eyes. A strange look.

And then the flash. Sudden and brighter than the light streaming from the sun. And Kalian Pendek lying there. Upper torso black-charred. Head and left shoulder gone. Molecular dust.

And Satu pulling from within his tunic an outsized laser pistol. Wheeling, peering, but not firing. Seeking, but not aiming, as from the skimmer the three other men run. They, too, weaponed. They, too, not firing.

And Satu barking orders, unheard by me but understood by the seamen, they reacting automatically to the voice of command. Lifting, moving what remained of Kalian Pendek up, over, and into the skimmer. Moving from cabin to back onto the deck, still looking for—what? For something to shoot at, for something to punish.

The yellow Satu now speaking again, the others nodding and moving to operational points on the skimmer.

Then the skimmer moving from the wharf, no longer destined for Crown City. The direction is eastward, out to sea.

Then all is black—for less than a second.

Then Thumb turned on the lights.

He gestured toward the vid-screen. "We can see it again if you wish."

I shook my head. "Three times is enough. I'll recall every detail years from now."

"Your conclusions?"

"Mine? I would think yours to be more valuable."

Thumb grunted. He had been standing, but now he sat. *Poured* maybe would be a better word. Thumb was not as fat as some, but his external being was soft, and as he heaved himself into the contour chair he rippled. There is no better descriptive word than *rippled*.

"My conclusions can wait. How about your questions? I assume you have some."

"Kalian Pendek—"

"To eliminate confusion, you may call him Six."

"Six, then. What was he working on—his immediate job?"

"Nothing."

I repeated the word. So did Thumb. "Maintaining identity, that's all. A break, something all of you appreciate—right? A breather."

Breather. "I don't think I'd appreciate that kind of breather."

Thumb shrugged his fleshy shoulders. "Anyway, that's what it was. No assignment."

"How long had Six—"

"He'd been on Usulkan less than two months."

"Before which . . ."

"That is classified."

I nodded. "*That* also might be important."

"It's being looked into. More questions?"

"Who knows he's dead?"

"Satu—and the men on the skimmer."

"No one else?"

"No one. Including Jana, if that is to whom you are referring. Continue."

"Satu. Why didn't he fire? The camera which picked up the action—"

"The recon camera, for security purposes, in order to—" He flushed. "Sorry. I forget that you know these details. Satu, however, did not fire because he could see no one and nothing to fire upon. As to your next question, yes, we trust Satu completely. You may now ask the related question."

"Which is: have you made a *mistake* in trusting Satu completely?"

"Elaborate."

"Who best knows Kalian Pendek, his timetable? Who most easily could set him up? Who, in your words, buried all the evidence at sea?"

Thumb nodded. "But who, may I ask, immediately communicated the happening? Who covered his employer's nonappearance at a guild meeting in Crown City by some subterfuge or other? Who has been a loyal servant of Kalian Pendek for more than ten years? And who, may I ask, would be stupid enough to have himself vid-recorded in a setup situation?"

"Six was."

Thumb stroked the rolls of flesh under his chin reflectively. "You don't care much for Satu, do you?"

"I didn't know I was supposed to. There are a lot of people I don't like personally."

"I suppose you're now referring to myself. In which case, am I supposed to take affront?"

"What you're supposed to do is your business," I said.

He looked at me levelly. "As is what *you're* supposed to do. That's my business, too. As to your liking or not liking anyone in particular, that I do not concern myself with. You have your job to do. Just see that you do it. If Satu has acted incorrectly, you'll know how to handle things, I'm sure."

Puffing, he rose out of his chair and led me to the north wall of the room. The entire wall was a mirror. He faced the glass, but his eyes were not upon himself. They were fixed on mine.

"You're simply to maintain identity—and find the answers. That's the job. It's only logical. After all, who should follow Six?"

I looked from his eyes to the reflection of my own and the face below it. It was a strong face, that of a man in his early forties. Close-cropped hair, black with streaks of gray, low widow's peak, almost-touching bushy black eyebrows. It was the same face I'd seen three times in the past hour blown from its shoulders.

Thumb was waiting for a response to his question.

"Seven," I said without emotion.

CHAPTER 2

Find the answers, Thumb had said. Find. Discover. Uncover. Search for. Hunt for.

Very apt, since the name of the establishment is Hunters Associated.

Hunters. Hunting for—almost anything. During my time with the organization I'd sought a variety of items, living and nonliving. Sort of a bureau of missing persons-and-things. Sometimes strange things, on appearance not apparently valuable. But valuable they all were, in one way or another. Because somebody always was willing to sacrifice something of value to acquire the thing desired. Money. Life.

The assignment I had just completed had involved both. Money—plenty of it, in the form of some missing documents from the files of a warlord on Pitcain II, and in the form of good old cash which was the return price the warlord would have to pay if he wanted them back. He wanted them back—badly. They implicated him in a healthy pack of double dealings which, if exposed, would have earned him the deadly wrath of some other powerful people. Life, thus, was in the balance as well. And some lives were sacrificed before the warlord got his documents back. One of those lost was his favorite wife, a light green-skinned thing who was lovely to look at. Her part in the theft had been minor, but the lady died, nonetheless. It was a matter of necessity, in that she had a very nasty weapon in her hand at the time—and it had been pointed at me.

Hunters. I had been one for nine years (New Earth Standard) at the time Six cashed in. If his number had in fact been Six. I had only Thumb's word for that, and although he had no reason to lie, he had no reason to tell the truth either. I was—am—Seven. My number.

And my name. Except for some thirty "identities" strategically located on some thirty scattered worlds. Such as Kalian Pendek on Usulkan. Thirty-odd names, most carrying with them impressive titles and influence—and the kind of entree which assisted immeasurably in the work of Hunters Associated. Thirty-odd names and a number, the last my only constant "identity."

Because, other than that, I have no real name.

I had one once. That is, I admit, hearsay-conjecture which cannot be proved by me. But everybody has a name. Six, no doubt, had one, although no one on Usulkan or Dominique or Raven's Beak or anywhere else will mourn him by it. If he was mourned at all, it was at a time before he was assigned his number and became part of Hunters Associated.

Associated. With what? With one of the countless intelligence agencies of nations, worlds, the Federation, merchant guilds, religious sects? Or with one of the para-police or military organizations of these groupings of sentient things? Or none of these? Or, on a part-time free-lance basis, all?

The aides—one for each identity, as the yellow-fleshed Satu served Kalian Pendek—might know, but they'd never said. Those in a position comparable to Thumb's might know. If there were others in a position comparable to Thumb's. He'd never said that either.

What he had said, that first day—my first day—nine years ago as we sat in his office, was right to the point:

"I am known as Thumb. You are known as Seven. Welcome to Hunters Associated."

With which he produced a medium-size mirror. Into which I stared and saw a reflection that was—obviously —me.

"Where—"

"On the world of Bold Brannigan, member in good standing of the Federated Nations of New Earth. City of Kincaid, respectable enough—this district, at least. You're on the sixth floor of—"

"Who—"

"Seven."

"No. My real name. Who am I *really?* I don't remember."

"Naturally. You do not remember because you do not have a real name. None other than Seven. Now, shall we get on with your orientation to—"

My hands were flexed to wrap eager fingers around his fat throat. My powerful leg muscles were coiled to spring me across the short distance. Then I relaxed.

Thumb nodded at the thick straps that held my arms and legs. "I've found they are effective in reducing wear and tear upon my person at times like these. Now, let us proceed to your questions. I assume you have some."

I was to hear these words many times over the next nine years. I would come to know it as Thumb's normal manner of briefing. I always had questions, naturally. This first time was, under the circumstances, no exception.

"Who are you?"

"Thumb. I am your supervisor. In that I have no psychological needs regarding obeisance; you may address me simply as Thumb."

"My . . . supervisor?"

"I hold that position with Hunters Associated. You, Seven, hold a position that reports to mine."

"You keep calling me Seven."

"Because that is your constant identification."

"But who *am* I?"

"Seven."

"You know what I mean. Who *was* I?"

He shook his head slightly, in disapproval. "There is no need to raise your voice. I assure you, there is absolutely no advantage in it as well. To respond to your question, however, you—whoever you were—died."

"Died," I repeated.

"For a time, yes. Fortunately, your remains came swiftly enough into the hands of our organization and—"

"Died?"

He waved his hands. "I think so. But I must confess that I really don't know. Mine is not the medical expertise. You may have been only about to die rather than actually expired. In any case, you were rebuilt. You are no longer—shall we say—yourself." He laughed at his joke, then the lines of his face grew serious.

"But you are very much your present self. Your reconstructed body-mind complex has retained several of the skills you acquired prior to your—ah, renewal. Think of it that way. Renewal. As for other areas, considered by the medics to be defective or nonproductive, they have been eliminated and replaced. In addition, you have been given certain other advantages over the normal-run homo sapiens. One skill you brought with you—I may tell you this even though I'm not all that well acquainted with your personal case—is that of dealing death to others. You will see, it will come very natural to you."

"I'm supposed to kill for you?"

Horror flashed across his face, feigned or not I couldn't tell. In the subsequent nine years I never once learned to read Thumb any more accurately.

"Kill for me? Heavens no, my boy. Not for me, not for the organization, not for its clients. Of course—"

"Yes?"

"You may find yourself in a situation—occasionally, mind you—where you will have to kill for yourself. Self-preservation, as it were."

As it were! Thumb was an expert at understatement, it proved out. But at that point in time, that first meeting, there were so many things to learn:

This firm—

Hunters Associated. It locates things clients want.

Why me?

You were available and considered adequate.

This face—and my body . . .

Rebuilt to specification. "Why? Don't you like the way you look?"

"Compared to you—"

"Respect, Seven. A little respect, please."

And there was the big one, the question that had been forming in my awakened mind for some time:

"Suppose I don't want to work for your outfit? What then?"

He smiled. "What do you think? I am certain you have a thought or two on the subject."

I did. Whoever I had been, I could think real straight now. But Thumb said the words first:

"Kill you? Is that what you think?" He laughed. "Seven, my boy, consider. The organization rebuilt you. Obviously that kind of medical miracle costs more than a little money. It would not cancel a project such as you—excuse the word *project* but that's what you are, an item of capital investment—and accept such a loss so willingly. Now and then we do lose an operative, mind you, but certainly not by *choice!*"

I grinned nastily. "Then what's going to hold me to you—to playing the number Seven to the fattest Finger I've ever seen?"

He rose. "It is true that I'm somewhat rotund, which is why I shall overlook your remark which, after all, is no more than sound observation, albeit expressed in a rather insubordinate manner. But my girth—as I prefer to label it—is a direct result of the same cause which will influence you to remain in the firm's service. Actually, my boy, I'm going to release you from your bonds in a moment, and if you wish you may walk out of this office, never to return, and the organization will not lay a finger —or Thumb—on you for the rest of your days."

He ended his little speech and looked self-satisfiedly into my face. He was waiting for the next question. I'd be damned if I was going to ask it.

But I asked anyway. "This—influence you mentioned?"

He turned and pulled a briefcase from his desk. He opened it and sat it on my lap.

"I assume you recognize Guild notes? Let us consider this your first payment—one to accustom you to the easy living you will be enjoying in the days ahead. Of course, you must sign for this advance."

He closed the case and produced a voucher and a pen.

"You *did* recognize them as Guild notes? I am correct in that, am I not?"

He was. A moment later my freed hand grasped a thin pen rather than the fat neck it had been yearning for earlier.

"On the bottom line," Thumb directed, peering over my shoulder to make sure I got it right. I did.

Seven, I signed.

CHAPTER 3

Aram Faan, I signed on the passage slip. The slightly-built milk-white Davidite female checked it and me respectively against the signature and tri-D photo in Aram Faan's Federation passport and smiled.

"One way to Juang Luar," she confirmed. "Can we be of any further assistance to you?"

Flashy smile, sexy eyes. I wondered just how much time I had before lift-off. If in fact there would be enough to . . .

"Hotel arrangements? A ground-vehicle, perhaps?"

I shook my head. "I believe my people have arranged all that for me in advance. But thank you."

"Perhaps I can book you through for the next part of your trip. I assume there is another leg, since your ticket is one-way."

Aram Faan, chief executive of a munitions complex on Bold Brannigan, replied that there would in all probability be a next leg, but that he wasn't sure at this time what or when that would be, that it would depend upon the outcome of Juang Luar negotiations. Actually, Aram Faan would not be leaving Juang Luar for a while—not until a native of that planet named Jonothon Evvers, an

16

insurance investigator, returned from a round trip to Usulkan. Evvers, of course, would make the trip, both legs of it to and fro. He wouldn't spend much actual time on Usulkan itself, however. Because somewhere between Crown City Spaceport and the Sub-Oceanic Transport offices his identity would become that of Kalian Pendek.

Not as confusing—or as difficult—as it sounds.

A computer network handled the details of assigning identities to the operatives from moment to moment, from place to place. How much juggling was required actually I had no idea, in that I had—and have—no idea as to exactly how many operatives there are. I suspect that all of us have the same physical characteristics. I know at least that all of us who switch to and from the thirty some identities I know about are identical. Of course, there could be another group cast in another mold filling another group of names and jobs. Or three or five or more such groups, molds, names, jobs.

Academic, really, unless you thought you had a chance to find out. And that was one of the things I learned from Thumb's briefing technique. You can ask a question many times. But, sooner or later, when you get no answer you stop asking—if you've got other things to do, and I did.

The point is, the system worked. The computer network worked—at least to the extent of not having two or more Arams or Jonothons showing up at the same office at the same time. At least, that's what Thumb had assured me.

"The women." He laughed. "They wouldn't know *what* to do!"

Oh yes, about the women. But I'll get to that later.

Aram Faan enjoyed the movie on his flight to Juang Luar, and upon landing, consumed a light meal (breakfast, I think) at spaceport. An aide by the name of Mata, a Romboid with four arms—each built like a saur's leg and expert at strangulation, as I have had occasion to witness—collected Aram Faan's passport and gave him one in exchange. The surrendered passport would be deposited in a small public voice-vault at the spaceport. The vault, rented year-round by Mata, was keyed to and opened at Aram Faan's voice, however many of it there were.

Jonothon Evvers spent three hours in the first-class lounge, reading four news magazines and swallowing half again as many Gin Blue Drops. (They really know how to make them on Juang Luar, at least in the larger cities.) He then boarded *The Song of Irth* and deep-slept the length of the voyage.

He was more than refreshed when he exited from the Crown City customs stall, paused before a voice-vault, spoke, and placed his passport inside. As he closed the panel, a well-remembered voice came from behind him.

"Welcome back to Crown City, Mr. Pendek," the little yellow man said as he handed me my identification papers. "You've had good fortune on your trip?"

I looked into his slit-eyes, eyes I now wondered if I could trust.

"Better fortune than I had here, Satu."

"That is, of course, why you *are* here, is it not? To straighten out matters?"

I nodded curtly and handed him my bag. He was right on target, and I liked his way of putting it. The *matters* to be straightened might well include his scrawny little carcass.

And as the hovercab moved southward, I wondered how all the other Kalian Pendeks felt about him. Not just Six, but all the others. We were supposed to be very alike in our natures, in our mannerisms and reactions, in our likes and dislikes. Often I'd wondered how those other Hunters with my face and body, those men who differed from me only in their number-names, felt about —well, about anything.

Take the various identities we used. Which were their favorites? Why? Was it the position—the status of being a shipping magnate as opposed to being a theatrical agent? Or would the agent's continual access to weird and wild people and creatures hold fascination for some and not for others? Or was it maybe the places in which the various identities were headquartered? On a rating scale from one to ten where would most of my look-alikes place Crown City—or Kincaid on Bold Brannigan or Robertsville on Dominique? And why would the choices be made as they were?

And the kicker question:

Would all the answers come out the same?

Thumb always had avoided that one, even when he was at his most communicative. "You are identical in many ways with the others, Seven. Obviously, that is what makes the system work. But there is such a thing as individual nature, the result of one's own peculiar experiences—happenings which are shared with no one else. But, tell me, why do you concern yourself with this?"

Once I answered his question with another of my own: "You tell me—do the others concern themselves with this as well?"

His answering look was totally noncommittal, which matched his answering words. "I do not speak to the others of you, Seven. I do not speak to you of them."

Fine. Maybe for the average man, but I am not average. There are times when—

You know the term *déjà vu?* It refers to a feeling you have that you've done something before or that you've thought something before—in exactly the same way you're doing or thinking it now. It's an eerie thing, and there are a couple of very sound scientific explanations regarding precisely what takes place in the brain when it happens. But when it happens, science doesn't help all that much. It's unsettling, to say the least.

I've experienced *déjà vu*. Me—a man with a memory that goes back only to a quarter of my natural life. What's more, I've experienced something else, something similar, but something very few men can feel. I'll have this thought come to me, any thought—in fact, any action. And the end of my spine gets suddenly cold, and my whole frame racks with a sudden shiver. Because the thought I have is this:

Is somebody else doing exactly what I'm doing—*right now?*

"All right," I said. "Now we can talk. No—wait." Moving behind the huge marble desk in Kalian Pendek's office, I rolled from its side a plush "visitor's" chair, exchanging its position with that of the "executive" model that normally housed the president when he occupied his office.

Housed is precisely the word, although *enveloped* is as suitable. How the other Hunters reacted to it, I had no way of knowing. Whenever I had sat in it, with its extreme cushiony surrounding wingbacks, I felt a strong touch of claustrophobia coming on. Built to specification we all were, but this chair always served to remind me that there might be some differences, regardless of how subtle.

"Now we can talk."

We could, because the thick-walled and windowless conference-room-sized office was totally bug proof.

"It happened so quickly," he began.

"Blasters operate that way, yes."

"But you saw the vid-tape—"

"In which case, you should be telling me something I don't know."

"But I know no more! One moment we were standing there, on the ramp. The next and—and the *event* took place. When I turned toward what I believed to be the source direction, no one and nothing was there, nothing but a group of packing crates not large enough collectively to hold even a Suryan dwarf. No one and nothing, sir

—and as the tape showed, it was the right direction. The others saw nothing as well."

"Speaking of whom . . ."

"The captain, Garth, and the crewman named Seraso assisted me in securing the remains. Both have accepted early retirement and are happy to be living the good life on a remote pleasure island in the Southeastern Sea."

"The other crewman."

Satu shook his head. "I could not be sure about him, his silence. Fortunately, before I had to come to what would have been an unwelcome decision, an accident aboard the skimmer . . . Sometimes the fates assist."

Sure, sometimes. I was certain that the fortunate accident consisted of a seaman's clumsily attracting a six-inch blade between his shoulders.

"All right, Satu, where would you suggest I begin?"

"You are thinking of working tonight? Here in your office?"

I glared at him. "Any reason I shouldn't?"

His eyes didn't flinch. "None, except that perhaps you first might wish to freshen yourself."

I reflected that my skin did feel a little sticky and that my mouth tasted like a nico-tube processing plant. As I rose from my chair, Satu pressed the binding on one of a hundred or so leatherlastic books on the wall shelf to the right of the main office entrance panel. The shelf rose into the ceiling. Beyond it, through a thirty-meter corridor, were Kalian Pendek's personal apartments.

Beyond it, and beyond the corridor, was something else too—within my apartments. Something—someone—living.

A slightly glowing heat-filament above the inner panel told me that. I looked around for Satu's confirmation, but he was no longer with me.

Before pressing the open-button, I removed the stun gun from its hiding place below the button and turned the dial to a full, killing-level charge.

If she had been standing instead of curled up on my bed, things would have gone badly.

"Some greeting," Jana said, looking up from her magazine and smiling sensuously at what, under the circumstances, was a stupid crouched and ready-to-blast stance.

I lowered the weapon and stood a little taller. "Lose your clothes?"

The nude girl nodded eagerly. "Some sort of charity. For the needy. I trust you might be in a charitable mood as well? I hope so. I'm needy as hell, myself."

"I ought to clean up first."

"Later. We'll do it together. After we do something else together. Kal, please—it's been a long time."

I considered the proposition. Rather, I considered Jana of the blonde hair, dark eyes, slim aristocratic face, and perfect long-limbed body. I considered—the entire time it took for me to shed my clothes.

About Jana. About her and the other women. I did say earlier I'd mention them. All right.

Them. One to an identity, a fringe benefit to the job. The equivalent to the spaceman's girl in every port. Not that there weren't other girls on Usulkan; there were, but they were accidental. With Jana, what would Kalian Pendek want with another woman? From personal testimonial, the answer to that one is nothing. Not only was she a lover, but she was a lover in love with Kalian Pendek.

Sure, you say, but how did she feel about making love to so many *different* Kalian Pendeks? Answer: she didn't feel anything about that, because she didn't know about that. Even in lovemanship style, we Pendeks were assembly-line, it seemed.

Sure, you say again, but—but how did I feel about her not being *mine*, but every other Hunter's as well? Answer: Kim, Tandra, Umber, Etcetera. These being the other girls at other ports. I always had one nearby, and always she left no room for wistful thinking about that other girl, far away in another bedroom on another world. A further tribute to the abilities of my employers, yes.

"Yes," Jana said, after the immediate togetherness activities she'd programmed. "Very special. Your first night back. Do you wish to pick out our dining and dancing spots or shall I? Never mind, I've already decided—as I've decided what you'll wear. My evening things are here, so all that remains is to select for you. . . ."

She chattered on, a woman happy to have her man back on the solid earth again, a woman who took pride in her man's body as she dressed him, a woman who knew his apartment—and its contents—almost as well as he did himself.

Himself. I always had marveled how our "system" could fool a woman as feeling and intelligent as Jana. A thousand little things mark one man's behavior from another's, and yet—we got away with *this!*

I was thinking these thoughts, watching Jana rummage through my jewelry case, watching her close it slowly, a mystified look on her face. Then watching her smile brightly—as if her eyes were saying "Of course!"—and sliding across the room to the clothes I had discarded on the floor at the foot of my bed.

Again the mystified look as she lifted my tunic. Back now to the jewelry case, she extracted a platinum pocket fob and clipped it onto the inside of my breast pocket. About half the size of a human fist, pocket fobs were "in" things men's-fashionwise. They served absolutely no purpose other than decoration—and perhaps ostentation. The one Jana had selected was expensive but quiet. She stepped back and took an inspection-type look at it —and me.

"Kal. This last trip of yours. Did anything—anything bad—happen to you?"

I watched her eyes closely. "I don't know what you mean."

"I—I guess I don't either," she said in a low voice. Then she brightened again and stayed that way. Through dinner and through an hour's worth of nightclubbing, after which she insisted we return to my apartment. When we arrived, for one moment—only one—her eyes lost their glow.

"Kal, you do love me, very much. True and honest?"

"True and honest," I replied. Because to be with Jana was to love her.

Herself again, she placed her tongue impishly between her lips. "May I suggest you begin proving it?"

I did my very best.

CHAPTER 4

Operation Convince turned out successfully, judging by the all-smiles attitude of my bedmate the following morning. I awoke to the soft humming of soft lips and the pleasant smell of woman combined with steaming caffeinello, black. I pushed myself up to one elbow and accepted the extended cup greedily.

"Good."

She mock-bowed. "I put a little *drim* in it. Satu says you have a busy day ahead."

"You also dressed yourself," I observed, tasting the bittersweet tang of the mind-expander. "A commentary of your satiety? Or dissatisfaction with my previous performance?"

"Neither. Merely a commentary on your busy day ahead. If your night is less busy, perhaps I can show proper appreciation."

At the moment I had no idea of what my night would hold. I told her so. "But since I'm my own boss, at least in that office out there, I can set my own working hours. As I figure it, I've got a half hour before paper-shuffling time. And, as the maxim has it, never put off till later what you can have right now."

"You'll muss my makeup," she protested.

"In all probability, yes."

She took the cup, following which we took each other. Kalian Pendek had a very rough life.

Kalian Pendek's very rough life ended in a blood-spattering death, I reminded myself some thirty minutes later as I unlocked Kalian Pendek's huge desk. I had sent Jana packing off to her own apartment, drained a second cup of caffeinello laced with *drim,* and took over the reins of Pendek's—my—business empire.

Sub-Oceanic Transport. A mammoth operation offering inexpensive carriage of passengers and cargo beneath the surface of Usulkan's great and stormy seas. A most profitable business, but not a monopoly, and that by choice. Sub-Oceanic could, of course, have forced any and all of its six smaller competitors out of the game. But there was no need, there being enough business for all. My firm was cooperative to the highest degree, in fact. A monopoly is easily taken over by the government; seven independent firms are not.

Not that Usulkan had the kind of bureaucrats that would want to take us over. Not at all. If all business were owned by the state, from whom would the government officials receive their healthy bundles of graft? Even after Federation membership. . . .

I thought about that. When I had last sat in this office, Sub-Oceanic was using its influence to fight Usulkan's joining the Federation, which is run from Primus

City on New Earth. There were purely business reasons, having mainly to do with interplanet trade regulations which would place bothersome controls on some of Sub-Oceanic's activities. But, more important, there were Hunters Associated business reasons. With Usulkan part of the Federation of New Earth, Kalian Pendek became yet another identity lodged within the Federation realm. This would increase the chances (still nevertheless remote) that our dual-plus identities might be uncovered. Not wishing to become too vocal, our strategy was to divide the several Usulkan states on the issue. Separate states—even the largest ones—could join the Federation, and still our operations could run as we wished merely by changing our headquarters location. But the strategy failed, no state wanting to be left out in the cold—or, more realistically, no state wanting to court the perhaps-bloody coup that resistance to majority-and-Federation inevitably would bring. The Federation has been known to play rough.

Did the Federation—through its Intelligence arm—snuff out Kalian Pendek?

It was possible. Assassination was rumored to be one of their more persuasive methods. But probable? I doubted it. Kalian Pendek was just one of several voices against them and by far not among the more vocal. But it was something to have the computers check out—sudden deaths of heads of state and business.

I punched Satu's code on the desk unit and explained what I wanted. Accomplishment number one. Next on the list was to go through my desk, not a chore I saw as being overly difficult since the business was not really run from this office but from Satu's and those of a number of general managers.

It was easier than I'd expected. The six drawers were naked—except for a small sonic gun which to my knowledge never had been drawn from its storage place but this morning as always gave me a feeling of added comfort.

I was about to relock the desk when I remembered the special compartment, a section between two of the drawers on the left-hand side of the unit. I'd never seen fit to use the secret storing place. I stopped in mid-shrug.

Someone else had seen fit.

It was an expandex file folder, cream-colored. There was one word handwritten in block letters on the tab. TADJUK.

Meaningless to me. As was the assortment of papers inside the folder. Several memos, directing the movement of equipment from mainland to undersea locations and between undersea locations. All dated within an eight-month period in the previous year, all were very routine seeming—except for the fact they were in a folder hidden in the secret compartment. There was one document, a large sheet of imitation vellum, that was folded in fours. Unfolded, it revealed a drawing of some kind of spherical building. An undersea structure, by the look of the supports, but the very detailed architectural rendering was different in several respects from the transfer stations of which the company had some seventy on the sea bottom. New prototype? If so, still why so secret?

Unless it wasn't secret at all. Maybe it slipped from the upper drawer and went into . . .

Wrong alley. The drawers and compartment were sealed. No, it hadn't got into its hiding place by accident.

TADJUK.

What the hell was I doing? Was my brain malfunctioning? There was a simpler way to get my answer than staring at a word that I didn't recognize.

Satu answered my come-in-now buzzer promptly.

"Tadjuk," I said. "What does it mean?"

He repeated the word. His face was blank.

"Here." I showed him the file tab. Maybe I'd mispronounced it.

The face remained blank. "No, sir. I've never heard the expression used."

I passed the drawing across the desk. "Recognize this?"

Satu shook his head. "Where—" He stopped. "Mr. Pendek, are you feeling all right?"

As a matter of fact, I wasn't. Nothing specific, just a kind of fuzziness. A sort of slight loss of perception, like the edges of images and thoughts had blurred a little.

"I'm fine. Get somebody up here who might recognize—"

And then the edges blurred more than a little. I was only slightly conscious of my face-first splash onto the marble desktop. There was a black hole and I was swept through, horizontally at first, it seemed, then vertically down. Rushing wind pounded in my ears as I dropped down through and between the white crags jutting up to carve great holes in my guts. Avoid, that was the name of the game, but points were followed by points and I knew even in my blur-thoughts that it wouldn't be possible to evade every and all, and realizing that, accepting that— but no, I'd be damned if I'd—

The pain seared through my right arm and the pound-sound of the screaming gale rushed away from me and a demon hidden in the black depths is asking me about lacing my morning cup with *drim*. And I laugh like hell, admitting it because if that's the only sin of mine they've got on record, that's all to the good, although their lousy bookkeeping probably means lousy housekeeping in the guest accommodations. And there is a second shaft of pain in the arm, a needlelike—

Needle.

From the other side of my desk Satu examined the syringe, making sure the attached vial was empty. I didn't need clear eyes to know that it was. I could feel the lump in my shoulder, feel the hot fluid start inward toward my chest.

"That should combat the jackel-grain," Satu said. "The *drim* was loaded with it."

"I thought it tasted kind of . . ."

And then I took an hour's uninterrupted rest.

"That was very close," Satu said.

I looked skeptically at the iced crystal goblet he handed me, but my desert-dry throat needed something. The frosty beer was it. I drained the glass.

"Miss Jana . . ." Satu began.

"No, I don't think so."

"Ah. Then she did not serve you the caffeinello personally?"

"Ah. She did, but—"

"But a woman in love does not do in her lover? Literature would have it otherwise."

"So would real life." But he'd said the very same words I was going to.

"Yet you cannot believe Miss Jana capable—"

I cut him off. "Miss Jana is quite capable. Of killing, in addition to other acts, if she saw reason for it. The fact is—and I mean *fact,* Satu—that no woman who was about to put the final blocks to her bully boy would have acted—"

"Good word, *acted.*"

My fist bottom crashed onto the desktop. My face was blood red, I could feel the pounding heat. Whether it was rage or a reaction from the drug Satu had injected into me, I didn't know, but I felt myself slipping through the veneer of civilized human into the instinct realm of killer animal. I pressed my fist farther downward until the spirit passed.

When I spoke it was quietly. "We will have to check her out, of course. And the jackel-grain, maybe it can be traced. Have the lab analyze it."

"It is now being done, sir, though I doubt much will come from that line of investigation. Now, about the architectural design. . . ."

I noticed it no longer was on the desk.

"Vartris, our chief of mechanical engineering, is looking at it now, in the outer office."

I suggested that Vartris get his butt in here.

It was a wrong expression to use, I saw when the tall stalk-thin Clobis scrambled into the room on his four multijointed arm-legs. No need here to go into the niceties of the Clobian digestive-elimination system, but suffice it to say that—for sitting or anything else—a butt is neither necessary nor in fact present.

Unrolling the single antenna that held the drawing, Vartris smoothed it out on my desk with his two forearms, or legs or extremities. The two pale blue eyes set close together over his harelip looked down in the accepted manner, respectfully awaiting permission to speak. He got it:

"Well?"

"Yes, sir. Well, sir, this surely is an odd structure."

Look who's talking, I thought. I said, "Tell me something I don't know. For example, tell me what it's supposed to be."

"Yes, sir. Well, at first glance it appears to be similar to one of our deep water refueling stations. The shape of the main globular section and that of the outer hivelike structures connected with it by passage-tube, they conform to the general construction principles that—"

"That apply when building almost anything in deep water," I interrupted. "So much for first glance. What did a second glance turn up?"

"Differences, sir." Either our chief of mechanical engineering didn't recognize sarcasm when he heard it or he chose to ignore my tone. Probably the latter, whether out of an attitude of respect for position or one of superiority of mind, I'd never know.

"Several differences," he went on. "First off, the dozen arms extending outward from the central sphere. They appear to be more rigid than the usual fuel lines—more like off-loading tubes. Yes, very much so. But much smaller than ones we use for cargo. And these holding clamps at the outward ends of the arms. The drawing calls for swivels where they attach. Most unusual. All such devices I am familiar with normally have some give, to be sure, but basically they are fixed to hold their vessel horizontally. These would allow a ship to rest vertically."

"What's the advantage in that?"

"None, sir. Fast vertical acceleration puts quite a strain on the ship, as you might imagine. The ships in undersea service—except for the military, of course— are built with economy in mind rather than the ability to withstand such an improbable strain. Thus transport ship movement is kept as horizontal as possible."

Satu leaned over and rubbed his chin. "Undersea regulations call for a certain minimum spacing between vessels. Might not this vertical-hold pattern be one way to build a smaller complex and still load fuel within the rules of distance?"

The big blue eyes blinked respectfully. It was a good point, I thought. Correction: it wasn't.

"Not in this case, sir. If you will note the reinforcement components, you will see that this is not a small structure. As a matter of fact, it is as big or possibly bigger than our Helmedia terminal, our largest. Now, there are several internal differences I noted. Do you wish me to continue?"

I didn't miss the tone this time. The bastard *was* being smug.

I nodded curtly. "Two things before you do. One, have you heard the word *Tadjuk?* Two, sit down."

"Tadjuk, sir? No, sir. And I'd prefer to stand if you don't mind."

"I do mind." I jerked my head to the chair at the side of my desk. Creatures of his race have a most difficult time folding their legs in any comfortable position when forced to ocupy a chair built for humans. Cruel? Maybe. I was thinking that maybe it would take some of the smugness out of him.

It did.

Rather, the eye-piercing white flash that sizzled-hissed as his back touched the back of the chair—that took the smugness out of him, along with everything else.

The electrocharge left charred flesh and ash. And a white milk-curd cast to the once blue and alive eyes.

"Mr. Pendek," Satu said slowly. We exchanged glances, then our eyes went back to where they'd been fixed. Not on the dead chief engineer, but on the chair. It was the chair I'd moved from behind the desk.

Kalian Pendek's chair.

CHAPTER 5

AAA . . . NAME OF MOUNTAIN PEAK ON CONTINENT OF TAWON

BBB . . . WORD IN DIPURUAT LANGUAGE MEANING GREEN, THE COLOR

CCC . . . SIMILAR SOUND, DTACHTUK, MEANS TO SING ALOUD AMONG THE CREATURES CALLED YAGE

DDD . . . FAMILY NAME OF CROWN CITY JEWELER

EEE . . . ADOPTED NAME (AFTER MOUNTAIN IN AAA) OF LEADER OF SMALL-TIME PIRATE BAND, OPERATING FROM TAWON COVE

There was no FFF under the heading TADJUK on the

computer run Satu gave me. Five items, two of which—
the color and the loud singing in off-world languages—
looked unlikely. The other three, however—

"Satu, I want that mountain peak area surveyed immediately. Also as much background as possible on the
two men, the jeweler and the pirate. The mountain stuff
I'll need tonight—before the dinner hour. The personal
histories I'll want just as soon as you can get them to me.
As for right now, have my private skimmer ready to move
in five minutes.

"Destination?"

"Crown City. It's closer. Then to Tawon Cove, if
necessary."

Satu nodded. Going to the wall unit he extracted a
mechanism from one of the drawers and brought it to me.
"There might be trouble."

My eyes narrowed. "No more than I've had at home,
I trust."

Nonetheless I pocketed the maser knife.

The weapons alarm sounded in my office archway as
we passed through, and that in the elevator clanged loudly
until Satu touched the camouflaged panel that shut it off.
"Something's at least working right," I said. "Who's my
crew?"

"Captain Halley, Egarid, and Trow. We are especially
selective these days."

I knew all three, each a long-service employee, each
a veteran of the early undersea battles that helped Sub-
Oceanic establish itself as a successful enterprise against
pirate ships and raiders operating on their own or on
competitor subsidy.

As I walked the ramp to the waiting skimmer a slight
chill registered on my spine. Here's where Six had got
his. I looked where Six had looked before. Nothing.
Nothing except, higher up the wall of the facing company
warehouse, a small indention where the televiewer lens

was sealed into the solid, otherwise windowless, wall surface.

"Sir."

"Morning, Halley. Egarid, Trow."

"Sir," the two crewmen responded.

I stepped from the ramp to the deck and turned back to face Satu. "Two other things. I want that electrocharge traced if you can. Also the names of everybody who's been inside my office and rooms since . . . since that other accident."

Satu slightly inclined his head. "As a matter of course I have already initiated these inquiries."

"In which case you'll have no difficulty presenting their results along with the other items I've requested. Neatly presented with my predinner cocktail." Got all that, you cocky little bastard?

"Very good, Mr. Pendek." Flashing his little smile.

The thought struck me that I almost wished he was the killer I was hunting.

We were on the surface for less than ten minutes when Trow whispered something to Halley. The gristly old human captain looked sharply in my direction, curled his thin lips as if considering something bothersome, then ordered Trow to grab the wheel with one or both of his pincerlike claws.

"Begging your pardon, Mr. Pendek, but Trow says we've got a tracer on us. He says it ain't just an accidental scan, neither, but that it's been with us for more than fifteen seconds. I gave orders to evade-wheel if we can."

The zigzagging already had begun. I was about to ask if Trow's judgment could be trusted, then thought better of it. He wouldn't be serving the presidential skimmer if age had deteriorated any of his functions, including the special sensitivity of his species that enabled him to pick up abnormalities such as tracing beams. Trow was an Iurrel, of furry rodentlike face, short stocky body, and dangerously sharp hands and teeth. Iurrels were one of the four intelligent species native to Usulkan and the only one which walked upright on two legs like man. Lighter than a man, an Iurrel still was his match both in cunning and killing.

"Still with us?" Halley shouted at Trow.

A nod yes, at which Egarid, a black-brown Rim Worlder, left his engine monitor and asked the captain what was going on.

"Tracer. From shoreside. North-northwest of us, up ahead. Mr. Pendek, it could be connected to a gun of some kind."

Egarid doubted it. "The gun would have fired by now —before you started to shift pattern."

"Maybe," I said, "there's another explanaton."

"They just want to know where we're going?" This from Halley.

"Possible. More probably is that Egarid is wrong, that there is a weapon trained on us."

Egarid, with the respectful lack-of-respect common to old sea hands, spat over the side of the rail. "Then how come they ain't blown us out of the water?"

"Simple. They know the skimmer's moving but they don't know if it's worth shooting at. In other words—"

Halley had caught the drift. "In other words, they don't know who's on it."

Correct, or so I believed. Even the most powerful scope couldn't penetrate the translux shield that formed the sides and top of the skimmer's covering. The view was one way only unless you were within less than a half-kilometer and viewing with the naked eye—a security feature necessary to protect company installations. There was, therefore, only one way anyone tracing our craft could be sure who its passengers were.

Trow shouted at us, "It's getting stronger—they're coming closer."

That was the way.

"Speed thirty, straight line from them to us," Trow said. "Three-ten degrees."

"Distance," demanded Egarid, checking the mercury bubble on the rear of the laser cannon.

"Three and a half K's, nautical. Speed shift to thirty-five—no, forty."

"Ready," Egarid said with a toothless smile. His mouth formed an O of surprise when I grabbed his wrist. The one attached to the hand about to turn on laser power.

"Not yet. If they've got a power sensor, they won't wait to fire."

"But, sir—they won't have nothing left to fire with!"

"That's not an acceptable solution."

Halley cackled. "Mr. Pendek wants to know who they be! So it's eel and shark until we do—aye, sir?"

"Aye, Captain. Eel and shark. Among the whales if we can."

Halley jerked the wheel, this time a full ninety degrees due west to the shoreward. Speed fifty. Then a cut to the north for about a space of two heartbeats, then west again —speed now at sixty. Now south, back toward where we'd begun.

"That lost them," Trow said, his nose quivering cheerfully.

"They'll have us soon enough," Halley shot back as the skimmer banked due west again. "But not long enough to draw a bead. I hope."

I hoped so too. Our speed said seventy-five. Just about maximum, but we needed all we could get. Sooner or later those on the other boat would realize what we were up to. And when they did—if in fact their purpose was to blast us out of the water—they'd make their move to cut us off from our goal.

"They're shifting south," Trow said. "Speed is up, too. Fifty."

They were on to us. "Distance?"

"Two and a half K's, little less," he told me. "Right out there." He pointed north-northwest.

"How about the yard?" I asked Halley.

"Two. It's gonna be close shaving, if they turn in-land."

"They just did," Trow affirmed. "Speed sixty."

I nodded. "All right. No unnecessary maneuvers—push this thing!"

As the skimmer shuddered up to eighty, I looked at Egarid. He grinned back, showing me his thumb poised over the laser-gun turn-on. He had the message before I'd given it.

"Yard ahead, sir!" Halley shouted. And there it was, the shipyard of three luxury liner companies. A dozen or so great vessels were anchored off-docks due west. The whales, among which the eel—us—would lead the killer shark which—

"There he is, Mr. Pendek!"

I followed Trow's extended claw. A speck of black skimming a course aimed at heading us off from the yard. "Egarid," I said quietly. "A near miss, if you can manage it."

"*Yessir!*" And before the acknowledgment was completed, the cannon was on and firing. Two bursts. "*Off!*"

"Right." Halley said calmly. And yanked the wheel hard to south, cutting speed to sixty.

"Lost us," Trow said.

At which a geyser of water sprang up northwest of us, followed by a second.

"Not too close, not too far," Egarid said from the cannon-scope.

"One more," Halley ordered. "After I turn."

"Right."

And again we shot off at seventy-making-eighty, and again the big gun burst, and again the shark rocked in a cascade of falling sea. Trow's reading showed the effectiveness of our strategy. At least part of it did:

"We'll get there first." That was the good part.

"Their laser's on, sir." You guessed it, that was the bad.

Halley spat with the wind. "You tell me soon's their follow-beam brushes us—hear?"

Trow heard. *"Now!"*

The skimmer almost stood up on its nose from the deceleration. "The game starts," Halley said through his teeth. "Trow, keep me informed."

And again we shot off, the nearest liner getting closer by the second—but close enough? All of us knew, it would take only a second or less to—

"Got em!" Egarid laughed. He'd provided them another boat-rocker. Two more and we had placed the good ship *Orlinth Havenhold* between eel and shark. We were in the confines of the yard. Now the cannons would be useless. Now was when *my* game began.

"Get in dense and let them start to close, then let me off."

Halley's eyebrows jerked up. "Off, sir?"

"I'll tell you when. Let them see us."

He did and they did, then we straight-lined it full from them. Our speed was down to forty, but that can be plenty fast among closely parked whales, believe me. Halley spun the wheel in his big hands with seeming carelessness, moving in and out and between and a couple of times too close to the bigger ships' exterior paint for comfort. I had to tell him to slow down, not for fear of personal safety but for fear of losing our hunters. I wanted them behind us and seeing us making each turn—and not having to guess at our whereabouts. That might lead to their moving on an independent course, which in turn might lead to a possibly unpleasant surprise. Unpleasant for us, I mean. I had in mind executing an unpleasant surprise of my own, unpleasant for them.

Them. Who? If I found what I was looking for, maybe I'd know.

I found it. "Halley, that ship there—the white liner."

"The President Wirth?"

"That one. To the other side of it—from the left—then around behind it and to this side again. Close. That's what I want."

Halley looked to the point near the aft end of the liner that I indicated and nodded. Checking that the killer craft was in sight, he gunned our skimmer straight at the great jutting bow to the left of us. Spinning the wheel as we passed the mighty tower of steel looming over us, he shot along the liner's full length, cutting his speed to twenty-five, then twenty as we approached the aft.

"This is gotta be timed right, sir," he said as he started his next turn. That was no news to me. It had to be timed perfectly. We could not round the aft until the pursuer vessel had rounded the bow. That, unfortunately, would leave me precious little time to do what I had to do. But so be it. Hunters Associated had turned me into an almost perfectly coordinated being.

So prove it, Seven.

"Now!" Halley snapped, and we shot around the stern of *The President Wirth*. Almost instantaneously, it seemed, I had my hands on the steel cable dangling from the *Wirth's* first deck. A repair cable, it was, and as my feet left the skimmer deck it was my palms that, scraping along the thick ragged steel, felt like they were going to need some repairs of their own. As I brought my boot-soles flat to the shipside and yanked the cable outward, Halley speeded up the skimmer, still staying close to the side of the *Wirth* as instructed. Now all I needed were three pieces of luck.

One: that the shark would swing as close to the stern as we had.

Two: that they would spot our skimmer's position before they got too wide out from me.

Three: that their speed would be slow enough for me to gauge it correctly.

One, they came around close. Two, they evidently spotted Halley's position. Three, their speed was just right. Four—yes, there was a four, an item of risk-luck that I'd considered but didn't want to think about over-much—they spotted me. Just before I left my perch at the dive.

The dive itself was not all that I'd planned it to be. Not only was the element of surprise missing, but my angle of body thrust changed midway. This was, how-ever, by choice, in that I thought it far better for the mo-ment to leave off my intended attack on the scrawny old salt sitting behind the skimmer's cannon and concentrate on the bigger and younger heavy who was drawing a bead on me with a smaller and more maneuverable handgun.

Lurching oneself to the side in the middle of a dive is not the easiest of tasks for a nonprofessional gymnast. It beats hell out of the stomach muscles. But, then, so does a knee to the gut—which is exactly what Heavy delivered at our impact. Overall, the dive and landing had to be counted as successful, since our gut-to-knee collision sent both of us flailing to the deck in a full-skid crash to the opposite rail. In addition, it sent his handgun skittering in the same direction but through, and over into the drink.

"It's him—Pendek!" yelled Old Salt at the cannon. Correction: he no longer was at the cannon but moving closer surprisingly spryly, a small laser tube in hand.

I rolled, and gaining my feet at the squat, launched myself once again at the old man, right chop-hand swing-ing hard. Even before the breaking neck-crack registered fully in my brain, I had circled behind him and shoved him toward Heavy, who was just getting to his own feet. The old man's body missed the target but my follow-up boot-sole didn't. Heavy looked down painfully at his caved-in ribs, then his eyes rolled up to somewhere back in his brain and he slumped, his lungs strangled in his own blood.

Two of the enemy and two down. Bad. I wanted a talking survivor. Which left the third and last party on board, a nattily dressed man in his early twenties, who leaned casually against the control console. I considered the maser knife in my tunic but dismissed it. He already had his in a more accessible place.

"My name is Aroyo, Mr. Pendek. Kutt Aroyo."

He paused, as if I were expected to comment upon the name. I gathered I was.

"You've heard of me?"

"Should I have?"

He shrugged. "Possibly. No matter—please, stay where you are. You're pretty deadly, surprisingly so for a man of your position. I can't complain, though. Now, you see, I get all of the payment for getting rid of you. Which I do deserve. I've been waiting a long time."

"Who's making the payment? Just curious, you understand."

"Sorry. Wish I could help. The guy who contracted us is a middle man, that's all. I've got no idea who dreamed up the stakeout for you."

"The middle man—his name." Keep him talking, Seven. Just a little longer.

"Uh-uh. Wouldn't mean anything to you. Well, Mr. Pendek, I guess this is it. Sorry."

And he did look genuinely sorry—right before Trow, his wet contour rising silently from behind, slit Kutt Aroyo's throat with an open left claw.

CHAPTER 6

"You didn't necessarily have to kill him," I told Trow. It was the first anyone had spoken since we'd transferred back to the company skimmer. Halley and Egarid held their tongues, aware that their company president was not happy with the way things had turned out. They were also aware that the president could be a tyrant when he was not happy.

Trow was aware of that as well but he had an advantage. He'd just saved the president's life.

"I'll put this as respectful as I can, sir. I didn't necessarily have to kill him exactly half as much as you didn't necessarily have to kill the other two."

He had another advantage. His logic was faultless. "That was respectful enough, I guess. So I'll go ahead and give you the bonus I had in mind." The big harelip widened into a superior grin which he displayed for his captain and seamate. It returned to normal when I pointed out that his bonus would be exactly the same as theirs.

"Which just might be unjust to them, Trow. After all, neither the captain's steering nor Egarid's cannoning got anybody killed, which to me is evidence that they know how to follow orders." I winked at Halley, who laughed out loud. Egarid clapped Trow on the back.

"All right," I said. "Fun's over. Let's get on to Crown City."

Crown City. Capital both of Alpha Continent and of the loosely-knit national entities of Usulkan. Population less than a million, but even so combining the worst elements of larger metropolitan centers with none of the elements which redeem its bigger counterparts. Smelly, dirty, murderous, ugly. The four words are descriptive of both the city and its inhabitants. Government officials did not walk the streets after the twilight hours without their bodyguards. Shopkeepers, too, kept armed guards about the place—and kept weapons on their own persons, since now and then the hired protectors felt their services worth more than their already high wages.

Tadjuk the jeweler had two guards inside his meager-looking establishment. Tadjuk the jeweler was meager-looking as well, though well-fed. Once you've known Thumb, you can't really call anyone else *fat*. But Tadjuk came close. It was his frayed clothing and general unkemptness that gave him his poverty look—a look which did not accurately reflect his financial status, according to the report transmitted by Satu:

"Highly successful. Specializes in doing one-of-kinds for the wealthy of Crown City and elsewhere in circles where his fame is known. Not known to have any criminal connections whatsoever. Not known to have been outspoken for any political or social cause, no doubt a function of his not wishing his politics to enter into a potential customer's decision to purchase or not to purchase. From all indications, then, a purely economic animal possessing an adequate amount of skill in his craft."

There was in fact a certain amount of craft—or craftiness—in the jeweler's eyes as he greeted me.

"May I help you?" He smiled at me, looked nervously at Trow—the others were with the skimmer—then returned his glassy eyes to me.

"I hope so. Do you know me?"

He nodded. "Of course, Mr. Pendek. Who does not?"

"What did you make for me or sell to me?" As his eyes widened, I offered an explanation. "I ask this because I've had a bout of sickness recently. There is a period of time I can't account for."

"I am sorry to hear that, Mr. Pendek. I've sold you nothing. I'm also sorry to hear *that*. But perhaps if you care to look around—"

"You said you knew me."

"And who does not, I also said. You are a famous man, Mr. Pendek. Now, over here in this case I have something I think is just the—"

"You've never seen me in your shop, never had one of my people purchase something for me?"

Something in the tone of my voice made him shrink a little. "No, sir, I know that for a fact. I keep very good records and could check for you, but there's no need. Certainly I would have remembered doing business with someone such as yourself, Mr. Pendek. Now, may I interest you in—"

"Trow," I interrupted. "Do you have a lady friend?"

Trow grinned. "Friend, yes, sir. But about her being a lady, I—"

"Buy her a gift, an expensive one, and charge it to me. Not too expensive, though, you hear?"

Trow heard, and as I saw the item he selected, I wanted to ask him what it was. But I didn't want to destroy his bliss by asking what probably would have been a stupid question. I'd never been much on keeping up with the latest trends in jewelry—I wondered, were all the Hunters like that?—but, still, I couldn't imagine what the thing which Tadjuk now carefully was wrapping up in gift paper could be. It was a long golden needlelike device, sort of a cross between an elongated cone and a stiletto.

But if I didn't understand the item itself, Trow had understood what my gesture had been all about. That bastard Pendek really did appreciate having his guts saved.

At the wharf, the signal beam was flashing red on the communicator. I clicked it on. Satu's report wasn't much:

"There's just not much available on the pirate Tadjuk. He keeps himself a man of mystery, so to speak. His taking the name of the mountain supposedly stems from his desire to keep his own name secret as well as to indicate that he and his followers have the strength of that great rock. Actually, the band is very small and not at all troublesome to the big shippers—they've never hit one of our vessels, for example. Mainly they concentrate on the pleasure ships, stealing valuables from passengers and such."

"Exactly where in the Cove is he?"

"Don't know. He hides himself well. It is said that no one finds Tadjuk in the Cove, but that Tadjuk finds the seeker."

Maybe we could arrange that, I reflected. I told Satu what had happened so far, then gave him my projected itinerary for the rest of the afternoon.

"In addition to that other stuff I want with my dinner martini, find out what you can about a young man named Kutt Aroyo."

"And what time will dinner be, Mr. Pendek?"

I briefly considered the travel time to Tawon and back plus the time it would take to find and meet with the pirate chief.

"Late, Satu. Late."

We—Halley, Trow, and myself—left Crown City in a rented hovercraft which would cut down the travel time to less than an hour. Egarid was to stay with my skimmer plus arrange to have another ready for us when the hovercraft put down near the cove. There were some special equipment items I wanted on board that skimmer, and Egarid was to see they were all arranged for.

The afternoon sun was moving lower in the sky as we descended past Mount Tadjuk and landed. The skimmer was ready, and as soon as we left the dock, I checked out the special equipment. Trow stood behind me as I did.

"That's one big lot of transmitter equipment, boss."

I nodded. "I want each of them set at frequency intervals equally spaced and connected to one input speaker. Every ten minutes, I want the frequencies changed by just a hairline. Keep off commercial numbers."

"What are you gonna transmit?"

"Not me, Trow. You."

When the frequency was set, I gave Halley orders to anchor near to Cove-center. Trow began speaking the lines I'd given him:

"Kalian Pendek, president of Sub-Oceanic Transport, wishes to meet with Tadjuk of Tawon Cove. Kalian Pendek's skimmer flies a white flag and lies centrally off the three shores. Tadjuk should reply on frequency one-four-three-zero. This is urgent. Kalian Pendek, president of . . ."

Five minutes passed, then ten. Then the change in frequencies, with the message repeated. On and on. Myself sitting in a deck chair with a small hand-sized transceiver, set on 1430, waiting. Halley sitting on the rail watching the boats moving about the cove. Trow hoarsely repeated his lines. Ten more minutes, another change in frequencies.

"You think they'll respond?" Halley asked.

"You got a better idea?" I asked.

"No. But I'm sure getting sick of hearing our fuzzy-faced friend back there."

"So am I. You give it a try, Halley."

His face paled. "Me, sir?"

"You, mister. And that's an order."

A dejected Halley was soon replaced at the rail by an unraveled-looking Trow. "I'm sure glad I never decided to go into the broadcasting business," he croaked. He poked a finger at the transceiver. "Nothing?"

"Nothing yet."

He turned to Halley and shouted. "Louder, Captain. I'm not sure they can hear you!"

Without doubt Halley's swear-words reached a multitude of tender ears. Hopefully, they also reached some ears which were not so tender.

We were counting time by segments of ten minutes now. A short rest for Halley as the control knobs moved, then back at it again. As the old salt's voice began to give out, Trow nodded at me and went back to replace him. Two ten-minute stints later and they switched again. Trow rested a boot on the rail, looking out at the fading sun.

"Odd, boss."

"What is?"

"That one little boat off to our right. She's been there for some time. Pleasure boat, looks like."

"And what's odd about that?"

"If we had the right kind of scanning equipment on this thing, I'd be more sure, but looks to me like nothing much is happening up on deck, except somebody just sitting there—looking our way. No fishing lines out. Odd. You didn't notice it?"

I'd noticed it, yes. The boat had ambled out at slow speed and tossed anchor more than thirty minutes previous. What's more, I also noticed something Trow did not—could not because he wasn't out on deck at the time. Two little glints of light, very close together, glints such as the reflection from the two lenses of a pair of binoculars.

"Keep your eyes on the boat," I said to Trow. I noticed then he had taken from his pocket the gift he had bought at the Crown City jeweler's. As he carefully unwrapped the package, I was about to ask him what in blazes the thing was. About to.

"Hold it," I said. "Tell Halley he can close down shop."

Trow looked up from his package out toward the boat. The figure cutting through the water toward us with a steady crawl was obvious. He relayed my instructions to Halley.

"The pleasure boat, sir?" the captain asked.

Trow's eyebrows furrowed. "There's what you could call a lack of communication on this here ship—with all its goddamned transceivers. Anything else you eagle-eyes think I ought to know about before the gent in the water gets here?"

I looked at him speculatively. "Only that the gent in the water is no gent, but a female. And based on just the quick observation I had a chance to make as she dived from her boat, I'd say she was a very shapely female."

When she was closer I saw that her young face was pretty as well. The full body I couldn't see, since she remained in the water, responding to my invitation negatively.

"No, Mr. Pendek. I am instructed not to come aboard."

"What are your instructions, then?"

"First, to determine if it is Kalian Pendek seeking to meet with Tadjuk. Second, to inquire why."

"I am Kalian Pendek."

"I recognize the face. Now, as to the second part—"

"That's for Tadjuk's ears alone."

She paused for a moment. "It is just a conference you wish? You do not mean any harm? Tadjuk has not, to my knowledge, touched any of your vessels."

"To my knowledge also. I ask only for a conference, yes."

"In that case you will come with me—just you. Your two associates will remain here."

I shook my head. "That really would be asking for it, wouldn't it? I'm the one who says who stays and who goes. That's final."

"Look, Mr. Pendek—it's you who wants this meeting."

"And you look, young lady. If this meeting doesn't take place—and fast—I'll use all the resources of Sub-

Oceanic to hunt out your insignificant little pirate and blot him and his merry men from the map. I trust you have no doubt that I can do it."

"My instructions—"

"You have just received your instructions—from me."

"Mr. Pendek, I'm sure you are aware that your broadcast was picked up not only by ourselves but also by the—"

"By the Cove authorities as well," I completed. "I understand that fully, as I understand your concern that those same authorities—who I have no doubt are eager to trace my skimmer's movements in the hopes of my leading them to Tadjuk—would not be welcome visitors to your headquarters. That is why the captain will stay with the skimmer and play decoy with whoever is watching. But this man"—I indicated Trow—"comes with me."

Her eyes followed mine. Trow was fiddling with the golden cone.

"All right, I suppose I have no choice," she said to me. To Trow she said, "That's very beautiful. I've not seen one so elegantly done."

"Thanks," he said.

As we moved to the seaward side of the skimmer deck and skipped into the water, I decided that maybe I'd ask the girl what the damned thing was. It seemed everybody knew but me. One thing—it wasn't a weapon, because the girl was firm that we should take no weapons with us. But she didn't blink an eye as, before both her eyes, Trow secured it in a zippered trousers pocket. And while her attention was occupied I pocketed something as well. Not a weapon, but something that might come in handy— especially since Halley saw the move in full.

Within a matter of minutes, however, I saw that the stricture against weapons was purely one-sided. The three men awaiting us, flat on their stomachs on the pleasure craft's deck, were the proud and no doubt capable possessors of three heavy-duty blasters.

"Just a precaution," the girl said.

"An effective one," I commented.

Trow grunted at the indignity of having to lie prone on the deck, but that too was explained as a precaution. "The attention of the harbor police will be drawn to your skimmer which—ah, it begins to move. Now we can do likewise."

Now, by the way, I had a full view of the girl's body. Her figure was more boyish than Jana's, but she moved with an animallike grace that was tempting. Very. But, even had other things been equal, this was one day I didn't have the time.

"A further precaution," she explained as she drew out of the cabin a light opaque canvassine tarp. After arranging it neatly over myself and Trow, she pointed out that the measure was precautionary in two ways. "We don't want anyone to see you with us. Further, we don't want you to see the way into our place. I'm sure you'll understand why."

Trow again grumbled, but I shoved the palm of my hand in his face.

"Shut up and just listen," I said in a low voice.

Soon enough there were things to listen to. Scratchings on the sides of the boat—tree branches—then sand scraping the boat bottom. The bow lifting up, then dipping dramatically down. Over a sandbar, into deeper water. More trees now, passing slower. Something of heavy wood creaking, water splashing with an echoing sound, the echoes getting deeper. Then—

The girl's voice reverberating as through an amplifier. "All right, the tarp can come off now. And you both can get up."

As we did, Trow caught his breath. We were in a high-ceilinged cave which nature, aeons ago, had carved into the side of some foothill of the great Tadjuk Mountain. The water surrounding us was pitch-black and still as the boat moved to the shallows of the rocky shoreline. The cave was lighted by means of wood firebrands, the flames flickering long and deep shadows in all directions. Along the shore were close to a dozen fast-moving vessels—and some twenty men, all weaponed. But the weapons were at ease. In here—in their own place—there was no reason to fear the lone outsider. Even so, as we stepped from boat to rocks, the girl felt the need to caution me:

"No sudden or threatening moves, Mr. Pendek. Your first will be your last."

"Which one is Tadjuk?" Trow asked.

"I am," came the response—from the only woman in the cave.

So much for Satu's data. *A man of mystery, so to speak.*

"Are you surprised?" she asked me, her tone and expression both those of amusement.

"Only that you took the trouble to bring me here," I said. "We could have had our little talk out in the Cove. That would have saved me quite a bit of time."

"Do you place such a high value on time, Mr. Pendek?"

"It's little bits of time which compose life, *Miss* Tadjuk."

She laughed. "Before we go any further, I wish to show you something. Over here."

Over here was near the far wall of the cave where a high chair had been carved out of the rock. That had not been the work of nature, but the men who carved it had lived long ago, as was obvious from the weathering which had taken place since. What was below the chair, however, was nature's work. It was fascinating, as was the pirate leader's explanation.

"It's a whirlpool, very swift as you can see. Anything caught in it goes down—and out. I have no idea where. As you can see, it's big enough for a man of even your shoulder-breadth, Mr. Pendek. Some of my men have attempted to swim in it—but only one or two have been able to get out afterward. Dead bodies placed there, of course . . ." She let the sentence hang.

"Your reason for telling me this?" I asked.

"Should be obvious, Mr. Pendek. Now, then, let us have our little chat."

She did not climb to the height of the rock chair, but sat upon what might have served as a footrest below it. Between us now was the whirling pool, and behind myself and Trow—

"I said I wanted to talk to Tadjuk, not to your entire clan. Tell them to go and polish their weapons or something."

She smiled. "You think I fear to do so?" Then she laughed and gave the order for her men to attend to other business. "Now . . ."

"It's very simple," I began. "Somebody has been trying to kill me. I'm just wondering whether or not it's you, and if so why."

"Kill you? Why—how is it you think it might be me?"

"The name Tadjuk came up," I said.

"There are other Tadjuks, possibly."

"There are. I'm asking about the pirate Tadjuk."

"You already have your answer, in that case. Mr. Pendek, if for some reason I wanted you dead, you'd be dead right now. Do you not agree?"

I did and told her so. "Which therefore concludes our conversation," I added. "We'll be going now."

"Not so fast, Mr. Pendek." I did not like the sonic gun which suddenly was produced in her hand.

"Our business is concluded," I said levelly.

"Not quite." She smiled. "You know that you are a very big fish, Mr. Pendek. A big fish which now happens to be in my net."

"I grant you that. But I also know that the only reason you're still in operation is that you've avoided big fish like me."

"Very true, but the present circumstances call for an alteration of basic strategy. You see, if I were to try to attack one of your vessels—regardless if I should fail or succeed—your punitive response would be the end of me and my band. I know of your ruthlessness, Mr. Pendek. All of Usulkan knows how you think and act. But this is different, far different. I have *you*—you yourself. Right here. Your company will pay a very large bundle of money for your safe return, I'm sure. What's more, they'll know I have you. Just about everybody with a radio heard your broadcast trying to contact me. All I have to do is put the word out that contact has been made, but that unfortunately you and your man are my captives. When you do not return to Crown City, they will have no choice but to believe me."

"You're still forgetting the eventual reprisals," I said. "They'll come—whether I'm alive to direct them or not."

"They'll come, perhaps. But I and mine no longer will be where we can be found. You see, the sum we'll be asking will be more than ample to fund us to a place—perhaps off-world—where we all can live the lives of ease, and privacy."

"You've got it all figured out," Trow said through his teeth.

"Quite so, sailor. I figured it out shortly after I first heard your broadcast. You correctly assumed that we monitor all shipping bands. Do you see any flaw in my figuring?"

Trow didn't. Neither did I. "Your move," I told her.

She looked from me to a point over my shoulder. "Wevar! Suss! take these two and bind them securely—yes?" Her attention returned to Trow.

"Ma'am, before you bind us up, there is something you could do for us."

Two good-sized men—obviously Wevar and Suss—were beside us as Tadjuk asked Trow to expand on his statement.

"Lunch, ma'am. I know Mr. Pendek wouldn't say nothing about it, him being real proud and everything.

But we haven't had a thing to eat since this morning. And as long as you're bent on keeping us here—"

She laughed cruelly, jerking her eyes toward mine. "So *Mr.* Pendek drives his men to the point of starvation, does he? Well, well. I'll tell you what, my rodent-faced sailor. You shall have the most sumptuous lunch the hospitality of my pirate cave can provide. As for you, *Mr.* Pendek, your pampered gullet can do without, for a couple of meals. Perhaps then your gourmet palate will find itself able to accept our humble fare. What do you say to that?"

"You've said it all," I said with a short bow.

Trow jerkily tried to follow suit. "Ma'am, I don't care what they say. You're a real lady. You're—"

It sounded as if an explosion had been set off in Echo Canyon. It was followed by men bellowing out cries for action. As for Trow and myself, we needed no call to act. Whether it was Wevar or Suss whose weapon my hand-blade onto his forearm caused to clack to the stone, I didn't know and didn't care. The point was, it clacked—directly after which he hurtled arms-flailing toward his she-boss. Out of the corner of my eye I could see the other heavy staring at Trow's claw buried halfway into his gut, but my main focus was on the girl, who was no slouch when it came to action herself.

Her first act was to blast her way clear of impediment. That meant dropping Wevar-or-Suss with a full charge to the midsection which stopped him halfway in his flight across the whirlpool. The water splashed to accept him, then gurgled over his head, both sound effects in the background to the main action, which was the girl's weapon moving around for her second shot. But the move never was completed, because, as alert as I was, somebody was even more so.

She caught it in the throat—that long conical golden piece fashioned by the jeweler who shared her name. Gagging, she dropped her blaster and brought up both hands to her throat. The fingers merely touched the expensive gold. Then she toppled from her throne, the pirate queen, clutching, falling—into the circle where rock surrounded fast-whirling water.

"No!" Trow roared. Then, seeing what he was doing, it was my turn to yell.

"No!"

But it was too late. He already was into the water, head-first.

He disappeared as quickly as had the girl before him. He was beyond help, at least he was beyond any I was prepared to give. Picking up the blaster dropped by Wevar-or-Suss, I ran toward the shoreline.

Occupied as I had been, I'd not noticed exactly what was happening within the rest of the cave. What had happened, simply put, was this. A tough-as-hell navy had followed the beam of the hand-sized transceiver I'd taken from our skimmer and had crashed the barrier at the entry way. This navy now had sunk three of the boats which had left the shoreline to do battle with it and was pouring deadliness all over the cave from its single cannon.

That's right, single. Because the entire navy consisted of a single skimmer, Captain Halley in command of both navy and firepower.

The first five men I dropped in rapid-fire succession are not much to my credit, seeing as how their backs were to me at the time. The next two I shouldn't brag about, either, because if they had been any good with their weapons I would have been a pile of dust indistinguishable from the other dust that lined the cave floor. One of the next three who took aim at me might have been successful, had not Halley lobbed one right in their midst. I took no chances and gunned into all three scrambling bodies.

Before I had a chance to direct my weapon anywhere else, I realized there was no one else toward which to direct it. It was all over.

"We've won!" came a triumphant howl from behind me.

It was Trow, holding his golden spike high above his head.

"You made it out of there?" I asked.

"Hell, boss—you heard the lady. She said a couple of her clods did it. If they could—"

"You could," I completed.

"Right. Besides, she wasn't a lady anyway. She was trying to take my little trinket out to wherever it was she was going. What do you say to that?"

"I say let's get on that skimmer and to the hovercraft. I've wasted enough time on a false scent. I've got to get back to the office."

"Er, boss?"

I waited.

"Can't we take a little time for—well, what I mean is . . ."

"What, Trow?"

"Well, I wasn't kidding around with that broad, you know? I mean, well . . . lunch?"

CHAPTER 7

Satu stirred the martini slowly and poured. It was good, as usual. Even the taste of the *drim* I took with it didn't take away from the good quality gin. I'd got as much sleep as I could on the hovercraft trip back to our building, but still . . . I had the feeling there was going to be a long night ahead.

Like I said, the martini was good. The quality of Satu's information was not:

"No spurt of deaths of heads of government or business. Therefore, I think we can dismiss the Federation as a factor."

"Don't dismiss so quickly. Not when the Federation is involved," I replied. "Continue."

"You asked as to who might have been in your office since—the accident. Unless someone has mastered the art of passing through exterior walls, I alone have been in your office. Plus the lady Jana, last evening. Of course, *she* is beyond suspicion. . . ."

"Go on."

"Neither the jackel-grain nor the electrocharge are traceable. Both are of the common variety, no variance with those obtainable from a hundred sources. Unfortunately, your would-be assassin has not much in the way of imagination."

Maybe not, but whatever he lacked in imagination he was making up for in persistence. "What about Kutt Aroyo?"

"Small-time killer for hire, background of burglar, cutpurse, and for a short time soldier of fortune. He gave that up when he found he didn't like the taste of gunning after victims who could fire back. No known affiliation with any political or intelligence group. No further useful information."

"And our mountain peak—from which I've so recently returned?"

The little yellow man refilled my glass before answering. "We plugged into orbiting weather satellite visuals going back a full year. Readout for the area turned up nothing in terms of activity. We also spectroed the visuals for possible mineral deposits. Nothing of value within the mountain nor in the surrounding region. Tadjuk

Mountain might be a mountain climber's challenge, but it would appear to have no other significance other than its name."

"So we're back to singing aloud among the Yages."

"Or something green."

Speaking of which, it was long past the time for my dinner. I ordered it.

"Will there be anything else?" Satu asked.

"Yes. You better have something sent up for yourself. I want to see that video again. My death scene. We'll watch it together."

So there it was. More than a full day on Usulkan and I was back to viewing the video I'd seen three times before. Accomplishment to date: zero. Except for the fact that I'd stayed alive after four attempts to make me otherwise. Four tries in one day. The number seven was supposed to have been lucky among the Old Earthans, but just how lucky could Seven get?

Luckier than Six—so far, anyway.

Stepping from the rear ramp . . . the bright sunlight reflecting from his shiny boots . . . Satu with briefcase . . . three crewmen on the skimmer. . . .

What good was this exercise in review doing me? What the hell was I going to see now that I hadn't seen before? I knew every step on the ramp, every facial expression of all concerned by heart—

By heart.

"Hold it. Take it from the beginning again. Freeze the frame when I tell you."

And for what seemed like the billionth time, Kalian Pendek stepped from the rear ramp of the building into the bright morning sun. His boots flashed in the blaze of light. So for a brief moment did something else. "Hold it right there. Freeze that and magnify his chest area."

There it was. Possibly of no significance, but just as possibly . . . My line of thought probably never would have taken this turn were it not for the jeweler Tadjuk. And there was Jana, too. Her reaction last night. Jana. . .?

Maybe, but that could be checked later. Right now—

"Satu, a Tadjuk question: What sings, not aloud but silently, and is not green but red?"

My aide looked from the frozen picture to me. "You think perhaps—"

"We won't know until we inspect the body. We leave now."

"Now, sir?"

I finished the last of my glass, noting with disapproval that I had hardly touched my meal. "Now. Surface travel will be easier by dark. Under the surface it won't make all that much difference. Is there some problem with my suggestion?"

"A minor one, sir. I did not think you would be—that is, I did not think the body would be of interest to any except the murderer and those employed by him."

"You destroyed—"

"No. The body is intact or, rather, what is left of it is. It is merely that I have placed a guard on the location. Naumum watches the place."

According to Satu's instructions, the surface skimmer was waiting and running. We skimmed southward under a clouded-moon sky for a little under two hours. Then, at a company above-surface warehouse, we transferred to a tri-man under-sea racer—a special model with heavy armor plates and a noncommercial company-developed dart-drive propulsion package. Then followed two hours more, traveling a straight-line southeast and into the depth of the Sea of Fangs—so named because of the sharp, up-jutting kilometer-high rock formations that afforded dangers to navigation as well as opportunity for ambush. These lichen-encrusted towers had see much death in their midst, for it was here that the last furious battles over sea control had been fought. Around their bases was a junkyard of loser vessels and loser bones, now a feeding ground for the sea life which felt comfortable in these depths.

I had been here before, of course, but this time I was hit with one of those strange *déjà vu* feelings as we passed down into the irregular rows of rocky spikes. I let it pass as a holdover from my morning's mind-wanderings under the approaching-death spell of the jackel-grain. Or let's say I tried to let it pass. At the end of that dream world was a large pit of blackness, a mammoth blot of smothering death. And in this *real* dream world there was waiting, below the crags, on the sea floor strewn with memories of past slaughters, a very real and mammoth blot of smothering destruction.

Naumum, its name.

Naumum. Not really a personal name but that of an off-world species. But effectively a personal name since the Naumum in question was brought to Usulkan by Sub-Oceanic on a one-of-a-kind basis.

Kind of a squid, but amphibious. Color: dark blue-green, although at this depth and in torchlight more like a blacker black than that surrounding it. Unusual creature in that, if isolated at birth—if sealed off from excess moisture—natural growth was inhibited. If sometime later suddenly exposed to, or immersed in, water, supernatural growth was the result. Naumum had been brought to Usulkan in a vial no bigger than my fist. At his present stature my fist was the size of the cornea of any of his three luminous eyes. Take your pick which; none was pleasant.

Naumum's entire presence was not pleasant, from the top of his domelike head past the five sets of upper and lower fangs set in one expansive eye-to-eye mouth to the four long and powerful appendages that served for holding, swimming, walking, and acts not overly pleasant to think on.

A very formidable creature, Naumum. But very docile

—normally. Very much akin in spirit to the ancient canines in the stories of Old Earth, but perhaps more intelligent. A "best friend" kind of relationship with its master, a loyalty that, given the proper order from the master, could be very deadly for an intended victim.

I was his master, as was Satu as well. Personally, on the two or three occasions I had been close to the creature, I hadn't enjoyed it. Obviously, a previous Kalian Pendek had not felt the same way.

Another pinprick in the perfect likenesses of us Hunters.

Satu and I left the dart some distance away from where Naumum waited. This was a precaution against the beast's attacking the vessel. His orders from the yellow man were to destroy anyone coming too close. There was little to fear from him once we were out of the ship, since his senses would identify us even through the thin depth-suits we wore.

At least that's the way it had been and the way it was supposed to work this time. And, as a matter of fact, the way our meeting began.

"Masters Pendek and Satu," Naumum's voice rumbled inside my helmet.

"Naumum guards well," Satu said, indicating to me the metallex coffinlike box half hidden by stones.

One of the giant creature's thick arm-legs snaked out toward the box. "Naumum guards what he does not understand."

"How is that?" Satu asked.

"Master Pendek. Is it not him in the box? Is it not him dead? You did not say it was when you put it and me here, but is. It has the death-smell about it. Yet Master Pendek is here with you and with me outside the box. With no death-smell. How can he be outside the box and inside the box at one time? Explain to Naumum. Can there be not one but two Masters Pendek?"

"It is difficult to explain," Satu admitted.

"I think there are two hims, and if there are two then maybe three or four or five. Master Satu, can this be? Are there two of yours?"

"No, just one," Satu replied. "I will try to explain."

"Fine," I said. "You explain while I take a look inside the box. Open it, Satu."

"*No!*" Naumum roared. "No look in box. Master Satu look. There is just one of him. I can trust him. Too many Masters Pendek to thrust. First Master Satu explain, though."

I then did a stupid thing. I moved slightly toward the box. Impatience, maybe. Definitely stupidity. I knew that when the great beast's roar of rage crashed into my eardrums:

"*You are the false master!*"

He attacked then.

Man, according to the weavers of the stuff of both legend and science, came from the water away back in his prehistory. He therefore adapted well to training which reintroduced him to his aquatic ancestral home. Naturally he had to have some additions to his structure, whether external or implanted, in order to function as well as he does on solid land, but when these were in place he did quite well. He could live in the sea, working, eating, sleeping, and procreating others of his species. He could also fight there. Not only his own kind, but the natural inhabitants of the depths. More than likely, if he knew his business, man won.

Saber-shark, war-whale, and python-bloater are three of the most vicious of the under-sea killers. Man has killed each with nothing more than a metal knife. But to my knowledge no man has faced a Naumum without a modern weapon and lived to tell about it.

I now faced a Naumum—a first-time experience. What's more, this particular Naumum was a Naumum in rage. In addition, he was a *fast* Naumum who gave me no time to unholster the weapon at my side. Before the full impact of his attack had registered within my system, one of his unfurled arms had struck me in the midsection, another following it to crack into the backs of my shoulders. The two blows succeeded in upending me, my arms dangling close to the sea floor, the two hands on their ends frantically searching for a weapon of some sort. I managed to wrap my fingers around a long jagged boulder which I brought up from the bottom just as I myself, wrapped in Naumum's arm as snug as a birthday present, was brought up from the same.

I had one chance, one only, as I saw the yawning jaws coming at me full speed. I hoisted the rock high and plunged it bayonetlike into the phosphorescent target that was Naumum's middle eye.

The reflexive shudder that came with the ear-piercing scream sent me shooting up over the domed head like a skydiver. It was the chance I needed. As I started down —this time in a more controlled manner—my blaster was trained on an area just below his bottom lip.

"Make a move and you're dead, Naumum," I said through my teeth. "Stay right where you are. I want to talk, not kill."

"I stay," Naumum whispered. Two of his appendages were busy removing the rock from his eye.

I came to a rest at what I felt was a safe distance from the huge beast. "Now what did you mean by *false master?*"

"I mean you. You are false."

"You mean that the real Master Pendek is in the box there?"

"I—" He let out a howl of pain. The two arms dropped from his face and I saw the flaps of tissue surrounding the ragged hole in his middle eye. It was pierced full. It would not see again. Neither would the other two.

I realized then what the last cry of pain meant. Naumum toppled over onto his side. Behind him stood Satu, a glowing laser pistol in his hand.

Twice in one day, death had been inflicted by "friends" when it was the last thing I'd wanted. Naumum, like Kutt Aroyo, maybe had some information I could hang something on. Maybe. And maybe not, true. But this made a grand total of five attempts on good old Seven's hide, and the Fates would not always be so kind.

Even so, a few minutes later I would have been the last one to kick Dame Fortune's butt. Releasing the combi-lock on the box, Satu lifted the lid and stood back. I looked inside. Strangely, I felt little emotion looking at the body of Kalian Pendek. Maybe not strangely. After all, I'd seen him die several times now, seen the *live* Pendek turn into a *dead* one. These were but the remains, what was left. A piece of capital equipment, Thumb might say, whose usefulness was past. Except that wasn't quite so. I sincerely hoped this nonsalvageable hulk would be useful to me.

As for emotion, I felt it surge through me when I took the thing from the shattered chest of the headless man in the box. The thing—the piece of stone and metal— was melted at the top, but for the most part was intact. I turned the bright red-jeweled pocket fob so that I could see the back of it in my torch. And I grinned.

There on the metal clasp was written, in no uncertain lettering: TADJUK, CROWN CITY.

CHAPTER 8

The fat little jeweler sat straight up in bed, his eyes wide with surprise. Very understandable. It was a little late at night—or early in the morning—for receiving guests in his small bedroom to the rear of his shop. Especially a guest who had kicked the door open.

It was also understandable that the two guards had reacted as they had. I dropped one with a stunner while Satu's loudly-cocked laser discouraged further movement on the part of the second.

"Mr. P-Pendek," the fat man said, trying to rise but not sure whether it was completely advisable. I followed his eyes to the stunner I still held, then holstered it.

"I'm in a hurry, Tadjuk," I said evenly. "You still say you never sold me anything."

"I say that, yes, because it is the truth. However, I would very much like—"

"Save the sales pitch. Instead tell me if you recognize this."

He was nodding before he held the pocket fob in hand. Turning it over and reading his mark, he continued to nod.

"Of course I recognize it. It is my work, a very expensive piece. But it is ruined. The top melted so—why should anyone do this to such a fine piece?"

"Anything else you notice—besides the melting?"

He turned the fob in his hand, hefted it twice, and eyed me warily. "It seems somehow lighter, as if—yes, here! Someone has pried off the back, quite sloppily, and replaced it with silver sealant. Here, I take off the catch and—*blasphemies!*"

"And what?"

"Here." He extended the back of the piece of jewelry. "Someone has *hollowed out* the stone, Mr. Pendek. This precious, expensive—"

"Never mind about that. What is that thing in the hollowed part?"

It was a tiny construct of small metallic filaments. I'd seen it before, on the way to Crown City, but I'd wanted Tadjuk to discover it by himself. If he had placed it there, he'd have been running for hiding by now. Scared men may lie, but they do not lie convincingly. I was convinced the fat jeweler knew nothing of the use to which his work had been put.

"It looks," he said, "like some kind of electronic—I really don't know. I've never seen anything like it."

"How about *this*? You ever see anything like this?"

He squinted at the tri-D photo I shoved in front of his face.

"The lady? I think—I can check, but I think she is the very person who purchased this item. A lovely face, sir. One doesn't forget a face like that. Really lovely."

As we headed back toward the wharf, I told Satu to arrange to have that lovely face waiting for me when we hit my apartment.

"Kal, will you explain *what the hell is going on?*"

Alone with me now in my office, Jana was mad. A good sign, I thought. Good for her. I sat comfortably in my office chair, my feet up on the desk. The messengers Satu had sent to fetch the girl had overdone things a little. They could have allowed her time to dress.

But then I might not have seen the contrast. Between Jana's reaction and that of Tadjuk's. He had been scared. She was raging like hellfire.

"Kal—I *demand*—"

I rose, walked unhurriedly to my apartment, and returned with a dressing robe. "Here, put this on. I don't want my attention wandering. Here's something else. Look at it and tell me what you see."

"It's the pocket fob I gave you, but it looks awful!"

"Open the back."

She seemed to be wondering if I'd gone crazy, then she set about doing as instructed. When the back was off—

"It's *hollow!* How could it be hollow?"

"There's something in the cavity. What is it?"

She held it to get better lighting.

"I—I don't know, but you can bet that I'm going to see that little bastard jeweler—"

"I've seen him already tonight. He had nothing to do with it."

Suddenly she got the picture. Or part of it.

"It—this thing—is something bad. Is that it?" Her voice was soft, her eyes soft too but turned from me.

"I've had one of our electronics people examine it." I had, although even he wasn't certain. ("It's been melted by heat, sir, but I think it's therium. The stuff that's often used in connection with an eye-trigger of the most sensitive kind.") I saw no need to go into that with Jana. I kept it simple.

"It's a very adept contraption which kills people."

Now her eyes were on me all right. "And you think I—oh, *Kal!* Now I know why you didn't wear this last night, why you were—well, different! You actually think I—I—rigged up this thing to—"

"No," I said quietly. "I don't think that at all. But somebody did it."

"Somebody . . ." she repeated thoughtfully. "Somebody close to you, close enough to have access to your personal things."

I took the fob from her, but somehow my hands stayed in hers.

"How horrible, Kal. To have someone close by who . . ." Her voice trailed off. I knew, and I knew she knew that I knew, what her following thought had been. I give her credit; she voiced it:

"Kal, if it is another woman, I'll try to understand."

The eyes she turned toward me were ready to burst into salt water and plenty of it. I did the natural thing—natural to me under the circumstances, anyway.

I kissed her eyes gently. "There is no other woman, Jana."

"Then who, Kal, who—"

"I don't know—yet." I had a strong suspicion nagging at the back of my brain, but it didn't compute. It *couldn't* be right. But there was nothing more I could do about it now.

That wasn't exactly true. I could have carried my search on to the next logical step. But I didn't. I didn't want to. Instead, I carried the business at hand on to its next logical step.

Violence with the threat of extinction does something for us Hunters' sexual urge, I think. Speaking purely from this one Hunter's experience, of course.

CHAPTER 9

It does not compute. Does not . . .

I should have been tired. It had been a full day and night. But there I was, flat on my back on my bed, a sleeping Jana by my side, and me unable to drop off. Daylight almost dawning, and my brain darting in and out of the primary question.

It did not compute, it made no sense at all. It couldn't—

But some secondary questions had sensible answers. The murder method was now plain. The mechanism within the pocket fob had triggered the weapon, positioned correctly to take off Six's head. Probably the automatically set blaster had been in one of the packing crates, its barrel adjacent to a handily-carved hole in the side, its muzzle throttled to eliminate flare. Removal of the crates at a later time would be easy. And even if Satu had discovered the means—including the jewel trigger—nothing would have been lost, not really. All Satu would know was how the thing was done.

Now that was known. Big deal. If there had been an intelligent assassin who could have been captured, that would have been different. He might have been persuaded to talk, to add something to my paltry collection of facts.

Facts.

Jana commissioned an expensive pocket fob from a Crown City jeweler. Fact. Subsequently someone had the internal structure of the expensive item altered. Fact. Motive: to take out Kalian Pendek. Fact. Motive for taking out Kalian Pendek: unknown. The responsible someone: unknown.

Facts.

When Kalian Pendek was back on the scene, that someone knew about it. Yet who would know about it so soon after—

One: Satu.

Two: Jana.

Yet Satu could have allowed Naumum to pull my plug permanently if he'd wanted me dead. Also Satu would know that killing one Kalian Pendek would bring another close on his heels. As much as I wanted to strangle the little son of a whore, I didn't think I'd be justified. Not for this, anyway.

As for Jana, I'd checked her out in the best way I knew. And so had the computers a long time ago. If her psychcharts had given any indication that she might . . .

The method. That was important. Methods, rather. Plural. Forget the pirates, they were a sidetrack caused by an unfortunate choice of name. They had not been out to kill Kalian Pendek, not until he stepped willingly into their lair. But the other times—five of them. A triggered gun, an electrocharged chair, a spiked drug, a bunch of hoods at sea, and a beast called Naumum. No, maybe Naumum was not programmed to—

Programmed.

A triggered gun, *automatically* set.

An electrocharged chair which, when someone sat in it, went off *automatically*.

A spiked drug which, when ingested, was *automatic* in effect.

But the hoods. They didn't fit. But the other three methods formed a pattern. The killer, setting up his jewel-blaster surprise, could not be sure that it would work—unless he kept a watch on the scene. He—

Unless he kept a watch on the scene.

That's what Kutt Aroyo and his merry men were all about! A sort of last resort, in case the automatic killers failed. Aroyo had said it: "I been waiting a long time."

I'll just bet he had. The brain behind this had set up his three traps—each based on a pattern of Kalian Pendek —and bought himself some additional insurance. But how many? Four? Five? Or more?

Walk softly from here on, Seven.

I shall, but who has walked before me?

One: Satu. Two: Jana. Three: anyone of high enough authority within the company to have access—

But that was nobody. Yet, somebody put that file in Kalian Pendek's desk. That mysterious file in the *secret compartment* of Kalian Pendek's desk. TADJUK, the file was labeled.

Labeled *by whom?* Deposited by whom? Who, besides Kalian Pendek, knew of . . .

No, it made no sense. Unless—

Unless. Let's say for argument's sake that Six had placed the file there. That he had done so because he'd gathered bits and pieces of evidence that . . .

No. If Six had known the significance of the word *Tadjuk*—had in fact written the word on the label—he would have made the connection with the pocket fob, wouldn't he? Maybe not. *I* had made the connection only because *I* had a dead Kalian Pendek on my hands. Six might not even have bothered to ever turn the fob over and look at the engraved name of the maker. I thought about that. If Jana had given *me* . . . And then another thought struck me.

Jana misunderstood my reason for waking her.

"I take it all back, Kal," she purred. "All that about you and another woman."

"Just one question, then you can go back to your dreams."

"Dreams are all right, but the real thing—when it's right here beside you . . ."

I asked her the question. She laughed softly and reached for me in a lazy but tempting movement. I asked her again.

"When?" she repeated. "I don't really remember."

"When," I said, my tone hard. "And it does matter. *When* did you give me that pocket fob?"

She sat up and rubbed sleep from her eyes. It's said that you can judge a woman's real beauty when she passes the line from sleep to wakefulness. Jana was beautiful; enough said about that.

"It's a hell of a time to ask, especially if your memory is so dim; but last year. About autumn last year. If you want the exact month—Kal, where are you going?"

"I'll be back. I've got to ask a computer. About something that otherwise doesn't compute."

Sub-Oceanic's computer was a dandy. A combination organic and metal thing, it was the largest of its kind on Usulkan and probably the dozen nearest worlds. Very expensive and very smart. And at this time this particular morning, very unguarded. I made a mental note to chew somebody's tail, and punched in my code.

"Good morning, Mr. Pendek," the computer said. It

was a female-sounding voice with a soft edge faintly reminiscent of the woman now in my bed upstairs.

I returned the greeting. "I have a file in my hand labeled *Tadjuk*. I'm going to read to you what it contains."

"I have already given you a printout on the word *Tadjuk*. Do you wish this repeated?"

"Negative. I know what it means."

"Excellent. I assume that the significance corresponds to one of the five possibilities I uncovered?"

"It does. I was getting to that."

"Don't. Not until I guess. I like to do that. It puts a little bit of gamble into what is otherwise a routine existence of data recovery and rationalization. Do you mind?"

"Not as long as you hurry."

"Fine. It was the jeweler, of course."

"Of course?"

"All right, in all probability. That's more exact, I suppose. *Green* and *sing aloud* I dismissed as being highly improbable. One would have to know those languages in order to be referring to them, you see, and I doubt that more than two or three people on this planet do. I could run a scan if you like."

"No need."

"As for the mountain peak possibility, I've already read the satellite records. Therefore, the jeweler."

"What about the pirate? There was a pirate also listed."

"True, but police data banks into which I am wired show the pirate Tadjuk's secret hiding place to have been raided. All were dead within the cave—it was a cave within a mountain abutting the Cove. Police are not certain which of the men found dead was the pirate Tadjuk."

"None of them was," I said. "Tadjuk was a woman."

"Really?"

"Really."

"Anyway, I was correct. It was the jeweler, right?"

"Right."

"And now? How can I help you?"

"I've got a bunch of papers from a file. Bills, consignment orders, things like that—and a schematic of some kind of building. I figure you can match them up with what you've got stored and tell me what it all means."

"I will give you a probable interpretation, Mr. Pendek. If you will place the objects in front of my visual scanner I shall ingest their contents."

The visual scanner was a thick piece of magnification glass in back of which was a series of organic optical parts. The staff referred to it as The Eye. The computer didn't seem to like the term.

"I see that you dismissed the guard, Mr. Pendek," she said.

"Wrong. No guard was on duty."

"That's strange unless—oh, of course. I see that it's tea time. Racklow always disappears for a few—ah, here he is."

I took the machine's word that it was Racklow entering the room. I saw that he was in fact carrying a small container of tea from a downstairs machine. I was not prepared for his reaction to seeing me. The tea container splashed to the floor. Behind it Racklow snapped to an on-guard *pa-kua* stance.

Throughout the Sub-Oceanic Building there are several areas which are most sensitive to light and heat. In these areas, one of which is the computer room, guards are not allowed to carry any kind of firearm for fear that in using it severe damage might be caused to things other than the intended target. In these areas, therefore, we employed a strange assortment of guards. All had one thing in common. Though they might carry cutting implements —for slashing and hacking but never for throwing—all were experts in one or more forms of unarmed combat.

Racklow looked like one of Satu's race, except he looked twenty times as large, his bulging muscles quite visible over and under the leatherette jock he wore. Like a *ki-sumo* wrestler, which I did not doubt for a moment he was. Shaved bald except for a thick black topknot, his slanted eyes regarded me coldly. A very efficient machine of death was Racklow, who had no business looking that way at the president of the company for which he worked.

"Something bothering you, Racklow?" I asked.

"You know my name. How?" The stance held.

The machine answered for me. "By the name of all those spirits you believe in, Racklow, you ought to recognize President Pendek. I told him your name. Now behave yourself before he discharges you."

"Maybe he's the president and maybe not. Use your Eye to check out the back of his hand. The left hand. Then tell me what you see."

"He *is* the president!" the machine insisted. "Not only did he code in that way, but I've got all his life-charges on file, and they check out."

"So check out the hand."

An audible sigh. "Mr. Pendek?"

"Left hand, back of," I said as I placed the required part of me before the computer's viewscreen.

Racklow still remained in his ready-to-attack stance. "All right. Is there a scar—a long jagged scar on that hand?"

"A scar?" The computer and I said it almost in unison.

"None visible," the computer continued.

"None," Racklow repeated. "All right, whoever you are, you'd better lift those scarless hands quick—and use them to defend yourself."

"Wait!" But there was no sense in wasting the energy. Especially since I was going to need all the energy I could muster.

His spring was more like a dancer's than an athlete's— a very heavy dancer, admittedly. It ended as his right foot stamped the floor and his left crashed into my right shoulder. It had been aimed at my chest—a real heart-stopper of a kick—but my dodge had been fast. Not quite fast enough, though, I realized as, following the impact, I spun around in a complete circle before colliding with the wall that had been, and again was, at my back.

Before my eyes had completely focused, Racklow's heavy hands had me by my jacket lapels and I was in motion again, this time without benefit of any contact with the floor—not until the trajectory I was in arced down and I made a skin-burning slide-landing which brought me in contact with both floor and opposite wall.

"Stop it!" the computer commanded.

I would have been more than happy to oblige. Unfortunately, it takes two to truce, and judging by the way Racklow was coming at me, he wasn't much interested.

I met his right-foot thrust with a left-shin parry and followed up with a horizontal sweep-kick, the object of which was to stuff my right boot-tip as deep into his inner ear as possible. But Racklow was good at parrying too— if he wasn't, he wouldn't have had his job—and all my boot-tip accomplished was the brief parting of his topknot. He had used his left forearm to deflect, and now he raised it to the roof. Right along with my right leg. The rest of me followed only partway when a downward chop of his right handblade connected with my own hastily-rising forearms.

Again floor and I met painfully. It was a lousy spot to be in, not just speaking generally, mind you, but with specific reference to the fact I was on my back while standing spread-legged above me was this hulk of a killer who had the superiority of position as well as skill.

"You didn't do too bad," he said with a smirk. Then he lifted his right leg—high.

I followed suit. I lifted *my* right leg high—and swift. My instep stopped with a soft thud high into his groin. As his smirk turned to something less happy, I was pleased to note that, even though I hadn't driven his private parts up into his craw as was my most fervent wish, I had nonetheless been effective. As a follow-up, I repeated my first effective blow. Then I rolled out and up and—

Hesitated.

His eyes had glazed over strangely. He staggered backward two steps. My hands were ready, but something was wrong. True, I had hit him hard, but not that hard where a professional like himself would feel he'd be finished. A ruse? A ploy to gain him some recovery time?

He held up his hands as I stepped forward.

"No. I am beaten. Let me expire in my own way. It is the least you can do for a defeated warrior."

"Expire? What in blazes are you talking about? I only gave you a couple of shots to the—"

"To the temple of my manhood. I am a Danchu, now humiliated. Thus—"

I've said he was fast, and he now proved it. From under his sash his hand whipped out a small but very effective blade. Its smallness I saw at once. Its effectiveness I saw after its pass by Racklow's throat. It was a very neat but deep slice.

He was dead before I reached him.

I turned to the machine. "What do you make of it?"

"A Danchu, he said he was. A very small sect, whose warriors cannot abide assault to—to what he referred to as the temple of his manhood."

A computer that was a prude, yet. "In Danchu martial-arts if one should foul another in that manner, he lost *his*—er . . ."

"All right. But aren't Danchus aware that us non-Danchus don't play like that? Especially when it's not a game?"

"They are so aware."

"And how about you—were you aware Racklow was a Danchu?"

"No, Mr. President."

"It's not in his profile?"

"No."

I considered that for a moment. Then changed the subject. There was something else bothering me. Racklow had me figured for an imposter because of the absence of a scar on my hand. That didn't make any sense at all. The organization knew well that, on a given assignment, any of its men could pick up some kind of wound. Normally, it was hurriedly repaired in a way that left no scar. But if that wasn't possible, if the trace of the wound could not be completely eradicated, then all of the Hunters got one to match. Precisely and very quickly. I wore two examples of proof positive on my flesh—one was a thick scar just under my right kneecap, the other a lightning-bolt-like slash on my right inner thigh. So it didn't make sense. Not unless, say, the last day of his life, Six . . .

"Question. You have the ability to recall all inputs and extracts from your system. Correct?"

"I can do that, yes."

"And you also can say who input what and extracted what? By name?"

"Yes."

"Excellent. When did I last come to you?"

"You don't remember, Mr. Pendek?"

"We're talking about your memory. At least I thought that's what we were doing."

"About six months ago. If you want the exact date—"

"No."

That was that. A blind alley. At least Satu might be able to respond to the question, but I doubted his answer would tell me anything. Then again it might. As for right now, I had some other questions, ones to which I could get answers.

"You are aware of all equipment purchases by the company and all deployments of that equipment, right?"

"Correct."

"Excellent. What unusual underwater structure has been going up during the past year? And where?"

"*Unusual* does not compute. Do you mean secretive? Unauthorized?"

"You have something unauthorized?"

"In a manner of speaking. There is a structure which has been built now which—"

"Which I have not authorized?"

"I did not mean that, Mr. Pendek. As you know, much construction work goes on which does not require your authorization. As a factual matter, the case I refer to did have your authorization."

"Then what do you mean when you say it's unauthorized."

"The government, Mr. Pendek. This particular project did not receive approval from the government. It was not submitted for approval."

"That's odd," I said. I was speaking more to myself than to the machine, but the computer replied to the point.

"It surely is. Especially when one considers the expense of the project, not to mention the company's firm policy of always doing business within the law."

The machine's voice had taken on the tone of a self-righteous old biddy. Understandable. It had no way of knowing that the Kalian Pendek standing before its Eye was not the same Kalian Pendek who supposedly authorized an unathorized construction project.

"Very well. What is the structure—and where is it located? And has it been completed?"

Now it was back to business, and the machine's tone matched the task at hand. "Purpose of structure unclear. I have no specfic data on the subject, and thorough scanning of total project input yields little, only that it is a reception-debarkation center much like those Sub-Oceanic already employs. Except for its size, that is. Location is some six kilometers straight off Needlepoint, and judging by the fact that no new requisitions have been placed for the site in the past four months, construction would appear to have been completed. Is there anything else?"

I looked down at the dead Danchu on the floor.

"Him. When did he come on the payroll?"

"About ten months ago. Interesting . . ."

"What is?"

"The fact that he was taken on by your personal recommendation, sir. Evidently you saw him perform. At least the personnel records show—"

"Great. I only wish I'd seen him take a shot between the legs before. It might have saved me some trouble."

"Mr. Pendek! *Is* there anything else?"

"I was going to ask you the same question."

"In that case, there is. A coded message has come into my central system. It originated from Bold Brannigan. Shall I decode?"

"No. Let me have it raw—on the screen."

The message was short:

ACT WARILY. YOU MAY BE YOUR OWN WORST ENEMY. THUMB.

Short and to the point. I was arriving at the same conclusion myself.

CHAPTER 10

"You're up early," Jana said lazily from my bed. Dawn was now full, sending its waking rays of sun happily over her pillow, caressing her dream-shedding face in a softness that tempted me strongly in what a Danchu would refer to as his bodily temple. Nonetheless—

"Up early and out early," I told her.

"You'll kill yourself working," she purred. "There's a better way to kill yourself. Let's make it a suicide pact. Come on back here. Your murderer and victim lies here waiting."

If I had been tempted to the point of yielding, her wording killed it. Murderer . . . victim. I was planning to make sure that he who was my would-be murderer would wind up as my actual victim.

"Uh-uh, girl." I punched a button on my bedside communicator. Satu answered in the middle of the first beep.

"Sir."

"I'll need my skimmer, and full diving gear for myself. In a quarter of an hour. That possible?"

"It shall be done."

When I had clicked off, I found Jana's arms suddenly around my neck. "Why not make it a half hour? You look like you could use some sleep, following a bit of special therapy. Besides, all work and no play, you know, makes—"

"Makes me grouchy as hell, but it's fifteen minutes nonetheless."

"Why don't we use my skimmer?" she suggested. "I've hardly had it on the water since you gave it to me almost two years ago."

"Uh-uh. You're not going."

She watched my face carefully. "It's something about what we talked about last night? The attempt somebody has made to kill you?"

I nodded. "The fly is going directly to the spider's parlor. Except I'm hoping the spider discovers he's bought himself a fly with a deadly sting of its own. Sorry, I shouldn't be talking to you like this. There's no need for you to worry. This fly is going to have quite a bit of help. Which reminds me."

I hit the button again.

"Sir."

"Satu, if possible I'd like to have Halley, Egarid, and Trow on the skimmer."

"I'll check, sir."

Ten minutes later, I boarded. Halley and Trow extended their good morning wishes.

"Egarid was granted a one-day leave," Satu informed me. "There would not be time to get him here, so I have substituted myself. I assume that is acceptable?"

"You'll do fine. Halley, the place we're looking for is about six K's straight off Needlepoint. Let's move it."

The skimmer moved, northward toward Crown City. Our destination was a long promontory sticking out into the sea from about twenty K's on the northward side of the capital. The maps called it Needlepoint, but to me it always had resembled a squashed index finger. The thin land mass itself was worthless, but the way in which it broke up the shoreward tide currents made the inland cove just south of the Needle an excellent tie-up spot for pleasure vessels. It therefore was a favorite resting and nesting area for the wealthy of Crown City, and on Needlepoint's more shoreward reaches a cluster of sea-motels accommodated the steady succession of rendez-vous, the secretive rooms necessitated by the fact that a sport with a wife on board his *Lucky Lark* could not very well bring a newfound friend aboard for anything other than conversational purposes. That the husbands fooled anyone was extremely doubtful, especially since during their absences their wives left on board did entertainment stints for newfound friends of their own. But that was their business. Mine was farther out to sea.

It was Trow of the furry face who snapped my attention back to the immediate present.

"Boss, it looks like somebody might be following us again."

Halley's gristled face gave me an expectant grin. "Maybe a little more action, sir—like yesterday?"

"Maybe," I said. "How far from us and where?"

Trow studied his spotter-sweep. "Three K's directly behind us. Could be coincidence, but after yesterday I thought I'd better mention it."

"Nothing trained on us?" Halley asked.

Trow shook his furry head no. "Like I said, could just be coincidence. After all, we're heading toward Crown, right?"

"Sir? You want me to change course?"

"No," I told Halley. "Keep it straight line, but push up our speed a little. Trow, you keep an eye on the follower."

We passed the shipyard where we had had our fun and games the previous day, then the Central Crown Dockyard went by us. The time of morning was now such that Trow's scanner was full of active little blips, early risers intending to get in a full day's work or pleasure on the water surface. As Needlepoint got closer, Trow reported that no single blip on his screen appeared to be straight-lining after us. "Of course," he added, "that don't mean too much. A zig here and a zag there . . ."

At a position ten K's south of Needle, we veered eastward. There was no sense in coming too close to the pleasure vessels of the cove, any one of which might be a lookout station for whatever it was I was going to find under the sea six K's out. So far we had stayed fairly close to the shoreline, but by my reckoning we were only going to be able to take the skimmer so close to our target before we would come into the range of its own underwater sensors. A secret and unauthorized complex surely would have them, which would cause us little problem until our craft was pinpointed as doing something different from others their scanners would show. Therefore the idea was to skirt the Needle at its southern tip and then to head straight out to sea—much like any pleasure vessel would do bent on getting into deep water as fast as possible. Then, at the point where our deep-sounders indicated we were over or nearly over target, our skimmer would leave something behind and continue seaward. That, at least, was the idea. It was direct and uncomplicated, but as it worked out it would have to wait.

No sooner had we begun our eastward move when Trow reported on the vessel following us.

"Sure looks like we've got ourselves a tail, boss." He beamed up magnification on his viewscreen, angled it in. "A skimmer, moving pretty well—small job."

"Can you get a fix on the pilot?"

He shook his head. "Uh-uh. Milk-glass screen, same as us. Although the flag she's flying is kind of strange."

"Flag?"

"Yeah. Red diamond with a *J* in the center of—"

"Let me see that!"

I saw it, then exhaled sharply. "You were right, Trow. *She's* flying the flag all right."

Satu smiled. "Give a woman a skimmer, expect her to use it."

"A little less of your inscrutable philosophy, friend." I said, my foul humor obvious.

"Directions, sir?" Halley asked.

"Slow it down. Satu, you and Halley run this craft through a few easy-to-follow exercises, but slowly put her back toward the yacht-yard. Keep Jana on spotter and maneuver yourself so that Trow and I will be in direct line between you. Got it?"

Satu nodded.

Trow didn't. "I don't—get it, that is."

"The heart of the matter, Trow, is that you and I are going to get wet." I moved into the cabin. "Come on—consider it part of the price of that trinket you bought your girlfriend. By the way, what the hell was that thing?" Finally, I decided to ask, flat out. Now, as we were about to visit my lady love, I had to know what one sharp-toothed rodent would buy another. He told me, flat out.

"It's a tooth-picker, boss. Damned handy when you've chewed a bellyful of them itty-bitty snails."

"Oh? And does your woman friend like a bellyful of itty-bitty snails?"

His eyes turned from mine. "Well—not really. But I do, so . . ."

"So—"

"So I kept the tooth-picker for myself. Anyway, it was too expensive a gift for somebody like her. It might give her ideas, you know?"

He grinned a toothy grin at me. For a fact, Trow's teeth had never looked better. Besides, the golden spike already had shown itself to be a handy thing to have on hand.

Inside the cabin, my outer tunic and trousers came off swiftly, leaving me wrapped in the tough but thin black deep-skin. Gloves, flipper-feet, and airpack were in place when I turned to see if my rodent companion was ready. He was, looking uncomfortable but ready to follow his leader. He pointed to the forward cabin seat.

"The secret way out?"

"No," I said. "Over the side is good enough. At this distance, she won't spot us."

To insure she wouldn't, Halley turned the skimmer so that it directly faced her position. We were over the stern rail and under the surface before he turned back to original course.

"She ain't going to like this much," Trow said over his face-mask communicator.

"She ain't supposed to," I returned.

You just don't hop aboard a skimmer which is moving along at thirty-to-sixty K's. Which is why I dropped the flare-shot across the *Lady J*'s prow. The craft immediately slowed, its anxious pilot peering over the starboard rail to see where the warning burst had come from. Her rifle at the ready—a dart rifle with which I had reason to know she was very good, having taught her myself—she was not long in spotting the lone black-clad figure who waved to her to approach. The circular wave was the commonly accepted signal for distress, and although a purist in such things might not agree, it was an accurate sign of what to me was pure distress.

Still, signal or not, Jana keep her rifle poised for action as she slowly steered her vessel to my place in the water. Very cautious woman, which in these days it was a good thing to be. Very cautious.

"Take off your mask!" she called across the waves.

I fumbled at the catch with one hand, holding the other arm low in the water as if it had been injured. I was stalling for time, until I saw that—

Ah. I lifted my visor.

"Kal!"

"I came to have a little talk with you, Jana."

She flushed in alternate shades of red. Then, with a hand-caught-in-cookie-jar expression on her face, she put her rifle down and extended a hand down toward me. "Come on board and we'll talk."

I shook my head. "No, Jana, we'll talk right here."

"That's silly, Kal. How can we talk—with you down there and me up here?"

"You're right, of course," I said severely. "All right, if you insist—come on in."

"Come on i—"

Her splash to my right was totally without grace. So was the way she spewed out the mouthful of seawater when her head emerged.

From behind the railing, Trow bowed respectfully. "No offense meant, ma'am, but orders is orders."

"Kal—" Her eyes flashed fire.

"Let's get out of the wet," I suggested.

I climbed up to the rail and stepped over it. Not waiting to assist the sputtering Jana, Trow and I headed directly into her cabin. The things I was looking for were on a side seat. As Jana reached the cabin door, I threw them into her path.

"I suppose you just happened to have these with you?"

"The diving gear? I always keep it on the skimmer. Always, Kal."

"Always right out in the open—and not in the handy storage locker provided for such equipment?"

"Look, it's *my* skimmer!"

"Correct. And it was following *my* skimmer. You want to tell me why?"

"You know why," she said softly.

I did. "And *you* know why I can't have you following me, not today. I thought I convinced you how serious this was."

"But I *know* how serious . . . Kal, I just wanted to help . . ."

"Thanks, but no thanks. You've already cost me some time, and that's something I might not have too much of."

Trow checked the starboard railside, then stuck his head back into the cabin. "Halley's coming."

"Good. Let's move out and meet him. Jana—you have any rope on board?"

Her tone was wary. "Why?"

"Answer the question."

"Well, yes—in the locker, but—"

"Get it."

She paused. Anticipating the fact I was about to repeat myself—this time a little bit louder—she went to the locker. It was a good length of good strong rope.

Ignoring Jana, I carried the thick coil out to the wheel. There was a glint of humor in Trow's eyes as he saw it.

"Take my lady friend to one of those fancy yacht clubs and leave here there. Then try to catch up to us. You might be needed."

"Aye, sir."

"Aye sir, *hell!*" Jana snapped. "Whose skimmer is this, anyway?"

"Yours, my love." I turned again to Trow. "Now, if she gives you any trouble at all, just use that rope over there. I sincerely hope you'll try not to mar any of her tender skin—which is truly dear to me—but if you have to I'll understand."

"Aye, sir. I understand."

"And you, Jana, do you understand?"

"Aye, sir," she said with resignation.

"Original plan, sir?" Halley asked. "North to the Needle, then straight out?"

"No reason why not—not now," I said, watching the minute speck that was now *Lady J* slowly get minuter to the west. "No reason at all."

But about three K's from Needlepoint's tip we saw plenty of reason for junking the original plan. We weren't going to get our skimmer out the further three K's.

The blockade was there to see that we didn't.

It was a flotilla of about thirty units—including several kinds of small vessels, some fast, others sluggish. But all of them had two things in common. All were heavily armed, and all wore the orange crest of the Crown Prefecture.

I did not need Egarid's reading to tell me that the skimmer moving out to meet us had its two heavy cannons zeroed in on our prow. And as we idled our engines and the Prefecture craft pulled alongside, I also did not need the cheery salute which came my way from the official-greeter type who appeared in command.

"Good morning, sir. I'm sorry, but these waters are temporarily sealed off by Prefecture order. It is therefore requested that you turn back."

"My name is Kalian Pendek," I said, trying to match his imperious tone.

"Of course, sir. I recognize the face of the president of Sub-Oceanic, naturally. But I have my orders, sir, nonetheless."

I gestured toward the other boats. "Some kind of problem? Underwater collision?"

He shook his head. "I am not at liberty to discuss the reason for my orders, sir. I'm sure you can understand that."

I could understand it quite well. Prefecture bureaucrats could be bought easily, and this was a case in which they were. Naturally, what could be bought could be unbought with simply a larger amount of identical currency. Also, one of Kalian Pendek's powers could save the sum and, even more simply, raise holy hell at the capital. But both methods were time-consuming, and I didn't have it.

"How far out does your sealed-off area extend?" I asked.

He smiled. "I'm sure that your man at the scanner can tell you as accurately as I can, sir. Now, if I may bid you a good morning and a happy cruise, I'd like to rejoin my other vessels."

I returned his happy salute with a halfhearted version of the same. "Turn craft," I directed Halley, then I went past the wheel and into the cabin. Before Halley's hand had pushed the throttle, my mask and breathing-tube were in place. Satu entered the cabin.

"Do you wish company, sir?"

"No, but keep in touch if they—" I jerked my thumb toward the seaward porthole.

"Normal frequency?" he asked. He was referring to the special channel we used from craft to the transceiver that was part of my face-mask. His question was a timely one, to which he already had anticipated the answer.

"No. Anyone building an underwater structure with Sub-Oceanic materials and with the help of the company's computer would be plugged into that channel." I detached the bottom part of the mask.

Satu manipulated the tiny dial and returned it to me. "You are ready?"

"Ready."

Satu removed the cushion and top frame of the forward cabin seat. To the casual eye, the structure I now crawled into was nothing more than a metal framing which could be used for underseat storage. It was more than that, as even the most casual eye could see once I was in full prone position and once Satu pressed the correct spot on the bulkhead. Before he did so, however, he brought me the two heavy-mass rocks which I clutched in my fists. Then he pressed the spot which brought the panel upward and over my back, sealing the compartment. Then the bottom section slid out and I felt myself plummeting downward.

The special compartment was part of several of our skimmers. The original purpose was to enable an innocent-looking vessel to stand by as it discharged and re-accepted an underwater saboteur who placed a charge timed to go off after the craft had leisurely moved from the spot. The ploy had been eminently successful, as veterans of the freight wars could testify. Now it was being used again, which was fitting—since this too was a war.

A different kind of war, to be sure, but war nonetheless.

CHAPTER 11

"Nothing," Satu reported. "No reaction. If they've got below-surface readers, they're not looking at them."

"Good," I told him. "May the good luck hold."

I still was dropping in the darkness, but now I activated

the red beam light which even in the darkest depths gave light to see by—if you were wearing the proper visor in your mask. I was, but still there was nothing much to see, not this far from target. I had about three and a half K's of swim ahead of me, the compass-depth-reader strapped to my wrist telling me which way to go. This would be the tricky part, getting through their spotters. There was no telling how far out they would be placed and in what pattern they might be placed. If in fact there was a pattern. The modern thing to do was just to rely on quantity, arranged in a helter-skelter format, the theory being that having no pattern stopped the opposition from figuring it out. Getting through without detection would demand all that good luck I mentioned to Satu. I had been in the water for less than twenty minutes when some of that luck appeared.

Although I wasn't sure of it on first glance.

In the seas of Usulkan there are several types of eels. I could recognize maybe four or five of them, but there was one type that every diver got to know real fast—the deadly charge-eel which dealt out its death in the form of a sputtering electric shock.

Fortunately the school of eels I saw were not of that kind. The large size was about right, but the coloring was a light yellow rather than the dreaded purple. Game-eels were what they were. Below and to my right, the twenty or so creatures were moving slow, but in the right direction. Joining them without causing them to scatter would not be easy, but if I could keep my movements flowing and quiet—

It was again lucky that I still was far from the school when my transceiver sounded off. It was Satu.

"Thought you'd want to know. We've rendezvoused with the *Lady J*. Bit of trouble, sir."

"Be explicit."

"Yes, sir. Trow was aboard, alone."

"As per my instructions," I said.

"I doubt if your instructions included his being trussed up as neatly as we found him. He also was out cold. The ship was left to drift."

"Jana—what happened to her?"

"Sir, the girl Jana—she was what happened to Trow. He says she got him when he wasn't looking."

I could almost hear Satu's following thought: Teach a woman self-defense, expect her to use it. But he didn't waste the effort. He got right to the point that was worrying me.

"The skimmer is positioned four K's from target. We're moving up as close as we can get without raising the security band. Then Trow will go under and try to find her. The problem is, we don't know how long her skimmer has been here. She might be past the point where she can be intercepted."

There wasn't much more to say, so I swore nastily. Then I told Satu I was breaking contact due to my joining the eels. "Stay off the channel, but find that girl, Satu."

He too realized there need be no further comment, signing off without a word. Damn it! Jana was a good swimmer, yes, but she knew nothing about dodging sensors. If they didn't find her and she triggered an alarm—

Damn it!

I joined the school of game-eels from below, making sure that I came in slowly and with no threatening move of arm or leg. Two members of the group inspected me with curiosity, but evidently satisfied themselves that I was no cuda or any kind of threat to their peaceful meanderings. They straighted, and except for moving to the side to widen the distance between themselves and the newcomer, slithered along as before. Most of the sea creatures behaved in a similar way. If a member of another branch of the tree of life moved among them, and did so in a nonviolent way, he was trusted—or ignored, which amounts to the same thing. There were only a few species of under-sea life that were duplicitous and they were recognized as such by the others. No cuda could get this close, regardless of how peaceful-seeming its behavoir. As for a saber-shark or a war-whale, its mere presence in an area of seawater was insurance that all other life had long fled—all that could make it, that is.

It was ironic that the most duplicitous of all life-forms —man—was accepted. The most duplicitous and the greatest killer-fish of them all.

Target was two K's away now as my compass told me that the school had begun to veer off toward the south. Just when I was going to need my protection the most, I was going to lose it. Unless . . .

Unless I could get them back on course—my course. And that might take some doing. But what the hell? I was sure that my friends and I already had registered on some kind of scanner. If that was the case, even if I scattered the school in my attempt to guide its direction, for a while at least I would appear simply to be one of those eels scattered—until they regrouped somewhere else, that is. Then I'd be one single blip, identifiable by my steadily— no matter how zigzagging—closing the distance between me and the eyes watching the scanner.

The southward movement was becoming more pronounced. If I waited too long to make my decision, I'd need to turn the school almost completely around, and that was a task that would be next to impossible. As a matter of fact, the job I had set for myself was next to impossible, but if I was going to try, I'd better get to it.

I got to it.

Moving to the front of the wedge was not at all difficult, due to the relatively slow speed of the school. The real problem was changing the course of the individual eel which was acting as pace-setter. This could be the eel at the most forward post, but not necessarily. The real director might be in the number two or three or four position. Attempting to swerve the point-man in that case would scatter the group just as fast as would a large explosion.

The precious minutes I spent simply observing after I'd moved to the front of the column were well worth the spending. The leader I wanted was third from the front, by far not the largest of the group, but he was obviously my man. The tendency of the two ahead of him was to move in a straight line. Twice he moved forward and brushed the rear-side of the leader. It was merely a touch, but my compass told me of the imperceptible shift in direction which resulted. I moved up and under the king-pin who had been directing the action up to this point, and with a very slow motion my gloved hand reached out.

The eel quivered slightly at the touch, seemed almost to stop in his forward motion. His head swung back to see what had caused the sensation to his body. Again my hand moved toward him.

At the second touch his tail-end arched away from my hand. But the movement was not violent. As it swung down again, I repeated my action for a third time. The contact was brief but firm. This time there was no arching response, not even a quiver. For an instant, I was concerned that perhaps game-eels do not give up their leadership positions easily, that my actions would be accepted as a challenge, the only honorable response to which might be a fight to the death. Some species reacted that way; whether game-eels did or did not I didn't know— the thought hadn't crossed my mind until now. Not that I worried about doing battle with such a creature. The steel blade I had at my side would be enough, let alone the maser-knife I also carried.

But the question was answered the fourth time I touched him. He edged forward and repeated the direction to the point-man.

Two more instructive signals and we were straight on course.

We were, according to my calculations, a little over

one K from target, when it happened. It came suddenly and completely unexpected.

The school scattered as if a bomb had been set off in its midst.

Why? I'd not been in the act of directing them when it happened. But then I knew why.

Below me and to the left front there was a sharp light —a red one, to be sure, but pointed exactly in my direction. Now with the help of my beacon I could make out the figure under the light source. A figure with a rifle-type weapon in hand. A figure coming up to meet me, swim-kicking powerfully.

I turned out my light, lurching over and deeper, drawing out my maser knife as I did so. The light below me blinked, then shifted places, but I could see it coming at me clearly. My weapon was aimed and ready to fire when I loosened my finger-touch on the trigger.

If it was Jana . . .

It wasn't.

Resourceful as Jana was, there were certain types of weapons she hardly would have access to. One of them surely was a fin dart with a warhead—and its own special red light. A very clever weapon in the hands of a very clever user. That blink of light I had seen was more than a temporary malfunction or repositioning. It had been one light going out—namely the headlamp—and another winking into action. Namely the thing I saw barely in time to dodge it.

But dodging was only half the game. If the firer of the dart was as clever as I figured him to be, he easily could have gauged the distance between us and set a timer on the—

The explosion caught me in mid-scramble to move from its source. It was powerful and bright and packed a wallop which I absorbed in my tensed shoulders. Knowing full well that the burst had silhouetted my form for the benefit of my would-be destroyer—wherever he was now—I overplayed the natural jerk of my body and let my arms and legs dangle as slowly I began to sink to the sea floor. I was offering myself as a perfect target for a second shot and I knew it, but I had little choice. He knew where I was, but I didn't have the benefit of a vice versa. The odds, although admittedly slim, were that he would figure me as being hit. That would make him less cautious. And seeing as how the burst-light was now gone, his lack of caution also might lead to—

The helmet light snapped on. He was a lot closer to me that I had thought—less than twenty yards—and coming closer, his dart rifle held at the ready. My movement still was downward slowly. If the Fates were kind to me, he would not notice the maser knife in my right hand until it was too late. If those same Fates *really* were kind in the extreme, already now my fast-approaching friend had made his report that he'd killed somebody sneaking around the area. If so, there would have to be a follow-up report as to identity—if it could be ascertained. If not—

And then I saw what my next move would be. In a flash I saw how I could get close to the structure I was seeking, the structure which everything indicated had to be very close now. With a whooping good deal from those friendly Fates, I might even be able to get inside the place without tripping any warning device.

He was less than ten yards from me now. All I had to do—

So much for all that talk about the friendly Fates. The maser knife misfired. More correctly, it didn't fire at all. Whether because of the shock of explosion or what, I didn't much care. The main thing was that, in whipping it up to the position from which it was supposed to do its deadly work, I had given the game away.

I now fully expected the dart gun to become active. It did, rapidly—which was fortunate. The firer had not chance to set a timer. The explosive would go off on impact only. A fast side-shift of my body saw to it that impact didn't take place as planned. The dart sailed past me and would keep going until it lost momentum. Then it would sink to the sea bottom where the little jar it made in landing would kick up a fair quantity of rock and mud. Fair enough, I had my own problems.

But so did my friend with the dart gun. I now was out of the beam of his light, to the left of him and above. As I came down, his helmet still was making rapid turns, a rifleman in search of a target. The speed of my attack was in response to that search, and to a second consideration. I didn't want him to have the time to make a report over the communicator I now was certain he had.

I was five feet from him when the red light dazzled my eyes. I closed the distance with as much power as my legs could grant, my arms straight out before me, my right hand now filled with a sharp blade of steel. But if he got that gun in position . . .

I laughed, realizing that he couldn't use the gun—not at these close quarters, not if the darts all held explosive heads. The laugh was short, but it shortened even more when the pain shot through my left bicep. Not all the darts carried warheads. Q.E.D.

I had been diving with the blade-point directed about ten inches below the light, looking for a fast throat-pierce. The hit he'd made, however, deflected my aim. Contact point was higher than intended. His light went out in a small hailstorm of shattering plastiglass fragments. With an extra push, I tried to drive the steel in deeper, but his backward and downward movement was too quick. In the darkness I felt his leg curl under my midsection and straighten. I went over him harmlessly.

Now it was my turn for some lighting tricks. With a quick pull I had my red light free from its housing. Extending it in my left hand as far from me as possible, I turned it on and began a fast scan. Immediately, there he was, legs spread and moving slowly to keep himself vertical as the dart rifle swung horizontally toward the light source which now, no longer being supported, was beginning to descend toward the bottom.

There was an instant where my form was silhouetted in my own light, but only an instant. Before the rifle could move to an interception position, however, my knife was lodged in a good six inches of skull. There was a short-lived spasmodic jerk, then the rifle dropped in the sagging hands of the dropped rifleman.

I collected my light, then collected the dead man. As I ripped off his hood, mainly to disconnect his radio, I gave off a spasmodic jerk of my own. It was one of surprise.

I had been little disposed to assess the man's weight and body proportions during the combat. These factors count a lot in unarmed battle, but don't mean much when you're facing darts with or without warheads. But now I saw—

One, the man was very light, very small in frame compared with myself.

Two, the dark cast of his face and the shape and absence of hair on his head showed that he was a Rim Worlder.

Three, there were a series of knife-cuts on both sides of his face. These were not random scars from some opponent's knife-blade. They had been skillfully done with the wearer's eagerly granted permission.

It all added up to something I didn't like. The only band of small Rim Worlders I knew about which identified itself with such tribal or clan markings was the Ku-Sidor, a people which the Federation had banned from emmigrating to any part of its domain.

Which meant that the dead man I was staring at was on Usulkan illegally. More than that, it meant that whoever brought him here had a bag of tricks which might be a lot bigger than I'd suspected.

I had been five minutes away from the first outer structure of the complex. It had to be connected to either

the main dome or one of the smaller armatures that I
had seen on the diagramatic drawing but none of which
could I now see in the murky waters ahead. But I was
directly on course, that I knew. It was a standard guidelight, pointed upward and at present not functioning. I
headed straight for it, using legs and one arm to move me.
The arm I was using was my left, which no longer contained the dart I'd taken, but still sent stabs of pain
throughout the length of arm and shoulder as I moved
it. But the pain would have been twice as much if I'd
been using it to pull along the burden my right arm now
supported.

As my feet touched bottom, I let the Ku-Sidor crumple
to the side of the guidelight. Then, extracting my knife
from it sheath, I began tapping the metallic casing of the
light. The message, in seaman's code, was direct and to
the point: *Have prisoner, am wounded, and coming in.*
The medium was metal-to-metal, and the practice dated
back to the trade wars when communicators malfunc-
tioned and a combatant returning to base had to identify
himself in order to get through without his own men turning him into a collection of scattered molecules. I was
taking only one chance, the way I saw it. The opposition
was sure to have a code prefix-word which was supposed
to be used in a message of this kind. But I was counting
on the mention of my being wounded and desperate, and
counting on the receivers excusing the missing code word
as a function of confusion or pain or both.

In any event, I could lose nothing by trying. I surely
was being monitored in their scanners now and there was
no way I could get to the main structure without them
knowing it. Secondly, I had another edge. What attacker
would drag with him a body of one of their own? All
things considered, the odds were that my story would gain
some acceptance at least within the complex. And even
if I couldn't get inside, the amount of plastic explosive
I carried with me ought to be enough to at least cripple

the operation. Cleanup could take place later, with a larger force.

My message tapped in five times, I returned my knife to its sheath and again picked up my burden. The angle of the connection where light housing met generator cable showed me my exact bearings. No reason to play cat and mouse now. Straight on in.

Thirty seconds, then forty. Then—there it was. Or, rather, there they were. And now it was clear why the docking devices were shown as they had been on the schematic. They weren't built for undersea transports, but space shuttles! Three of the dockers now contained ships, vessels which even in the hazy light of my red light clearly were heavily armed. There were no markings on the ships, none at all, not even registration numbers. In addition to importing illegal aliens, somebody was in the process of importing something even more illegal—a very potent strike force.

At the very least, I could defuse one of the strikers.

I had been swimming crippled-minnow style, and not only for dramatic effect. Unless I was now on visual— which I doubted in that I could see no red light source beaming on me from any direction—the movements my right hand was making at the top of my wet-boots would not appear unusual. Nor would my hesitation at the foot of the space shuttle ramp, in that it was a brief stop, as if I were catching my breath before going on to the nearest intake lock.

I didn't need much plastic nor time to plant it. The explosive material was of the type that would go off automatically fifteen minutes after exposure and attachment. Rip and slap, just two actions. Then, fifteen minutes later, bang.

A little more hurriedly now—like a man happy to be approaching a place where he could rest and be cared for —I headed for the nearest intake module. My plan of action now was firm. A piece of the stuff here, then swim for hell to the central dome, plant some there, then get out of range as quick as I could. It would be tight timing, but if my charges were placed all on the same side, I could get myself out of blast angle without much trouble. Unless . . .

I could see the main dome clearly now. It was of fantastic size, bigger than anything Sub-Oceanic had ever constructed. But, while the old saw about the bigger they are the harder they fall had always struck me as being nothing more than the false optimism of small men, it was true that the bigger an undersea structure, the more component sections to its exterior plating, and that meant that, regardless of how many cross-hatching supportive sections you used, the bigger you built the greater the inherent weakness of your pressure joints. So, anyway, was the song sung to me several times by the company engineers who continually delighted in telling their president why something he wanted done couldn't be, due to pressure loads, reverb buildup and other, more exotic reasons.

But first the intake. I was just about to strip off another piece of explosive when the top of the tank opened. It was an unusually large tank, which didn't make much sense. The larger the tank, the more air that has to be kept in the bubble chamber below. Very wasteful, unless you had reason to put a large group of men through at one time. There was another possibility, of course, but I didn't consider it at that moment. I didn't consider it until I saw it happen. But first I saw something else. The beam of a red light.

It came from high above, not from the direction of the dome, but outward. It was a small flicker, that of a swimmer who was just skirting the far boundaries of the complex. Before I could make any decision as to my next move, there was movement beside me.

The tank cover was moving on its hinge.

Crouching low, I was hidden in the mass of bubbles

released from the outsized neck of the module. So was what emerged. I did not get a clear look until it had passed through the tube and was heading upward toward the swimmer.

In the past hour I had seen an illegal alien and illegal warships. Now I was seeing something else. The rising creature was a Naumum, which on Usulkan was supposed to have been one of a kind—and very dead.

What was even more depressing was the next realization which greeted my eyes. The great black beast had not been the only being which had come from the module.

The three dart rifles were trained directly at my gut.

CHAPTER 12

I considered the possibility of resisting, but the consideration was brief, mainly because the resistance would have been brief as well. As I climbed up and then down through the open hatch, the three riflemen behind me, I knew that getting into the complex was going to be a lot easier than getting out. For a fleeting moment, I had the thought that once they saw who it was they'd captured, my position might give them cause for concern. But that thought too evaporated with the memory of what happened to Six and what had almost happened to me. No, the face of Kalian Pendek would buy me neither time nor sympathy here.

I was therefore taken back by the attitude of my three

guardians when, once we were through the bubble-lock, one of them stripped off my face-mask.

"Sir!" he said. He snapped to attention, as did the other two. "Sir, I—er, we—had no idea it was yourself—"

Their face-masks were off too and I looked hard at them. I did not know these men, but then the president of a company as large as Sub-Oceanic would not know all of the minions who drew their salaries from the corporation paymaster. In any case, the point was academic, since these men were not on the Sub-Oceanic payroll— at least the two of them who wore the Ku-Sidor tribal marks were not; I suspected the same about the third, a Suryan dwarf, whose initial shock at seeing my face was beginning to wear off.

"Sir, our apologies. But we received a report that—"

When the bull presents its horns, take them in hand if possible. An old saying among matadors on Dominique. The possibility seemed to be presenting itself. My voice was hard as steel:

"What kind of report was it that had you threaten me with—with those?" I stabbed a finger at the Suryan's rifle.

"Interlopers, sir. Two of them. We were told to release the Naumum for one and to follow up on the action. We had no idea—"

"Give me that," I commanded the dwarf. He looked to the other two for some kind of moral support, but received none. I tried to appear not overly eager to receive his weapon. When I had it in hand, I hefted it leisurely.

"The other so-called interloper—where is he being taken?"

One of the Ku-Sidors replied. "The Naumum will bring him to the tube and send him through. Our orders are to await him here. The Naumum is to remain outside, in case there are more—"

"*More!*" I broke in.

"Yes, sir. Again, our apologies for—"

But he stopped. Although all three had their masks off, the tiny communicators near the air intake valves still were operational. Suddenly they were operating. I couldn't make out exactly what was being said, but I didn't have to. It was enough that the message had got through to those for whom it had been intended. That much was fact—as demonstrated by the suddenly frightened look on the Suryan's face. The Ku-Sidors did not look frightened, but then they still had their rifles—both of which snapped up with unmistakable intention.

Both of which clattered to the floor as two darts from my weapon found their marks.

The Suryan dropped to his knees. "Please. I am unarmed."

It was a clear call for fair play on the battlefield. Coming from a Suryan, it was almost laughable. His race probably was unsurpassed at double-dealing acts of treachery. A case in point:

"I will do anything you say. I can help you. If you spare my life, I can be of great assistance to you. You will see."

"I'm afraid I won't see, although your offer is much appreciated."

"Sir?"

His eyes opened wide in surprise as my dart smacked home directly between them. The sound of movement in the passage leading to the outside whirled me around to face it. The business end of my rifle was in position. I lowered it as the figure stumbled into the chamber.

"Kal, what—"

"Not now, girl—we go back the way we came. Fast."

Jana's face was ashen. "But I can't. That—that creature out there. He ripped off my airpack."

Beautiful.

I pointed my rifle at the three dead men. "Try one of theirs on for size. They won't be needing them."

"Where are you going?"

"I'll be right back. There's something I want to leave behind before we take off."

I was through the inner lock before I saw just how optimistic that last statement was. It was Standard Operating Procedure for all underwater reception stations to have pressure readers installed in all armatures. These readers —a series of dials and control panels—showed at a glance what the air-and-water-mix situation was in that armature.

I glanced. The situation was lousy.

The reader showed beyond doubt that the exit I was planning on our using was locked up tighter than a drum. It also showed that the controls in this section were on central override. In terms of practicality, that simply meant that if Jana and I were going to get out of this place, somebody within the central structure would have to move a couple of dials. I doubted things were going to happen that way. Which left as our possible exits the other armatures fanning out from other sections of central—if they in fact were not all now on override and if in fact we could make one of them.

Too many if's. But I mentally added one more. If I could blast our way out of this one . . .

I went back to Jana.

"It works," she said simply, referring to the face-mask she now had in place. With reference to the dart rifle she'd taken up from the floor, she added, "I hope this does too."

I told her the problem. Correction: I told her half of it. A voice box above our heads interrupted me at about midpoint:

"You're sealed in, both of you. I would rather not blot out your lives before at least a minimum of conversation —especially with yourself, Mr. Pendek—but if I cannot help doing so, it will just have to be my loss. You both are being watched by vid-camera, so no move you make will take us by surprise. And before you can make any move, no matter how resourceful you think you are, I can turn you into jelly. Would you like me to tell you how?"

I already knew how, but the voice told us, anyway.

"Pressure in the tubes is controlled for a point just inches from where my hand now rests. At a touch of a finger, the walls that surround you can turn into an imploding coffin. An expensive coffin, to be sure, but effective."

"Kal—" Jana began.

I waved her to silence.

"Now, like good little boys and girls, kindly drop your weapons and walk—slowly—in the direction of the inner lock. Do you understand?"

"Kal—"

"You heard," I said gruffly. "Walk."

We walked. But as we reached the lock, Jana could not hold it back any longer.

"Kal, that voice. Didn't it seem familiar to you?"

"Jana, what I'm about to do is for your own protection."

"Kal?"

Her eyes showed a mixture of terror and mystification just before my handblade to the side of her head closed them in unconsciousness. I had no idea if it would really save her life, but this way the odds might be increased. Might be, that's all. Because, yes, I had recognized the voice on the box. Just as, a couple of passageways later, I recognized the smiling face which greeted me.

Thumb's coded message had been directly to the point. Both voice and face were, of course, my own.

"Power, my look-alike. I will have it one day—in undreamed-of measures. I trust the brandy is to your liking? Of course it is. If *I* like it, obviously you do."

The apartment to which he'd taken me was well-furnished. We were to have a "man-to-man" talk, he'd said, giving orders that Jana was to be placed under guard elsewhere. ("Clever of you to drop her when you did. Her having seen two Kalian Pendeks would be, as you correctly gathered, something I could not tolerate. In fact, I thank you for the service. She is a most pleasurable little piece, as you well know. Not only that, but in that she came all this way to try to protect you—me—is a virtue that should not go unrewarded.")

It was, to say the least, an unusual experience, sitting and listening to yourself talking. It was one thing to see yourself murdered on a vid-tape, but this, the in-the-flesh reality, was quite another thing. He seemed to share the same feelings. "You know, I never did get to see your predecessor close up—not like this. Truly remarkable, isn't it?"

"My predecessor—your successor, I take it."

He nodded. "Like all of us, very resourceful. I had no reason to have him killed, you know. Not until he began to gather bits of information which—"

He stopped. A red light on a console panel began blinking on and off. He pressed a button on what obviously was a communicator.

"Yes?"

The report was brisk and complete. The basic facts I already knew, of course, but it was good to hear the extent of the damage. The shuttle-ship was totaled. My fellow Hunter barked orders for all ships and hatches to be checked for similar bombs, then clicked off. When he returned his attention to me, he was smiling.

"Fifteen-minute plastic? Excellent stuff. I don't doubt that you've got more of it on your person, but there's no need for me to strip you—not yet." He shook his head, but still was grinning. "I should have known you'd plant an explosive somewhere out there. I must be slipping. All this"—he indicated his underwater domain—"it makes one careless. False security and all that."

"You were speaking of my predecessor," I said.

"Yes. It was most unfortunate, but if he began putting the pieces together too soon, well—" He frowned. "It is not a pleasant thing to have oneself killed, my friend. I did not especially enjoy it in the case of your predecessor, and I won't enjoy it in your case. Nonetheless, the deed was—and will be—necessary. More brandy?"

"Just a touch."

He filled my glass. He was not worried about my attacking him, the blaster in his left hand assured him of an edge, even if my wounded arm did not. Then, too, there was no self-defense technique I knew that he didn't also know. He had little cause for concern. But he was curious.

"Good old Thumb. He was fast in sending you here. But you were even faster. Two—three days, was it? Splendid. You're on-plant that short a time, and right into the heart of the matter. Tell me, how was it possible for you to be so damned fast?"

I laughed shortly. "When everybody keeps trying to do you in, speed is encouraged."

He nodded. "Once your predecessor had been taken out, I wanted to get that building cleaned out. The computer data as well as the death-traps. But my success at the pier was reported too late. By the time I arranged for the calling off of that Kutt Aroyo he was already among the missing. Your doing, I suppose?"

"One of the more pleasant aspects of the assignment," I said.

"I can well imagine. But, satisfy me on one point. How did you fit all the pieces together?"

Why not? "First, I don't have all the pieces. But I had a good start. That file labeled *Tadjuk*—"

He grimaced. "*In the desk!* Very stupid slip, leaving that around, but that particular evening . . . What happened was, I slipped into the building on an evening I knew—what was his number, anyway?"

"Six."

"I knew Six would be at a meeting which would last

hours. Therefore, I took the opportunity to return to him the doctored pocket-fob and to set up the other traps. The whole assassination operation, as you've no doubt realized, was code-worded *Tadjuk,* in dubious honor of that weasel of a jeweler. I had the file holder with some of the evidence, when that little bastard Satu—anyway, into the desk went the file. By the way, just to satisfy my curiosity, what's your number?"

"Uh-uh. That you don't get."

He shrugged. "No matter, really. Mine's Fourteen—or it was. I suppose you, like myself, have often wondered about your real identity?"

"It goes with the trade, I guess."

A wide grin. "What's not part of the trade is finding out. I did. A relatively simple method, once you figure it out. Anyway, that was the start of my thinking along lines which— Come, let me show you about the place."

His lift of the pistol told me it was time to rise. I did.

"One question first, though," I said. "How did you uncover your real—"

"No, my friend Hunter. That's a secret I think I'll keep for the present. Perhaps, just before I have to—but, no. I wish to show you things."

"I got the idea some time ago, but Usulkan seemed the perfect place to begin. The planet itself, with so much of its surface covered with water—an excellent place for me to start. Who would have figured that Usulkan would have given the nod for Federation membership? I didn't figure it, neither did Thumb, nor anybody on this world with any position of authority. Even so, it'll be a while before the Federation clamp is really firm on the surface, let alone the controlling of what happens beneath the waves."

Mastering the seas of Usulkan was but a first step in Fourteen's plan. No, not the first. He had begun accumulation of a vast amount of funds in several of our other, common identities.

"You know how it is. Money and how you spend it is of little concern to the organization as long as you do your job, whatever that may be at any given time. By the way, I suppose along with your true identity you also are in the dark about the true nature of Hunters Associated?"

He wasn't supposing. He knew the Hunters' situation from firsthand knowledge. I said as much.

"True; but knowledge of the second matter came with the first. I think, my friend, that you might be surprised to—well, that is relatively unimportant. Come, I want to show you things. You've got the kind of intelligence I know will appreciate them."

Among the "things" I saw, the general outfitting of the dome was not overly impressive. It simply was larger than others and held no marvels for the president of the company which was responsible for the design of most of what it contained. What was impressive was the cadre working within the under-sea installation. In addition to a number of Ku-Sidors and Suryans, there were a number of other species—which, if not banned specifically by race, I suspected were not welcome as individuals. Fourteen expanded on the theme.

"Most of them have some sort of price on their heads. Murderers, thieves, war criminals of various taints, all have a certain degree of technical ability. And all share the distinction of being hunted men. As a Hunter, I thought it only just that my shock troops should be composed of such."

"I take it loyalty is no problem."

He laughed. "Loyalty? That's something that is bought and paid for, as you should well know. Besides, now that they've been smuggled into this world, what would happen to them if I just suddenly turned them loose upon land? No, I have their loyalty, friend Hunter, even though I would not turn them loose. That might be dangerous to myself. Down here we have other ways to deal with the nonloyal."

I nodded. "I saw the Naumum."

"Yes. Docile creatures, strong of body but weak of mind. Sometime back I began experimenting with that other one—the one we brought in for the purposes of Sub-Oceanic—"

"The one I had to kill," I completed. "Your programmed computer guard is also dead."

"Programmed? Ah, you mean this?" He extended the back of his left hand to me. I'd already taken note of the jagged scar. "Yes, well, I thought it might be best to keep Kalian Pendek away from the computer—unless I myself wanted to use it. A tough one, Racklow. I selected him myself. How did you manage to kill such a one as him?"

"He's a Danchu," I said. "Or he was, anyway."

"And what, pray tell, is a Danchu?"

I grinned in spite of myself. "Somebody who can't tell his own crotch from the Holy Land."

He waited for a further explanation, then saw I wasn't about to satisfy him. His shoulders shrugged.

"And the Naumum, too, is it? That's really an accomplishment, my friend. Although he was an old one, wasn't he? Yes. Old also is the Naumum which was sent after Jana. We call him the Grandfather around here. But these—"

We had paused before a huge metal door deep in the maze of corridors in the central structure. "Fourteen," he said, and the voice lock clicked open. The heavy door swung inward.

"These we call our grandchildren."

Now I was impressed.

The circular room had smooth shiny walls which curved upward to form a smaller version of the great dome in which it was housed. In the center of the room was a complex of controlled air-supply vats from which tubing ran upward and then downward to—

The vu-thru cases numbered in the hundreds. Within them, in small compartments in a state of suspended animation, were tiny Naumum.

"About two thousand," Fourteen supplied. "Quite a navy of killer-ships, don't you think? Insulated from water at birth, they caused little transportation difficulty. But I call your attention to the electronic wiring connected to each of their cages. They're all being programmed— the way I want them programmed."

"Why so many? What makes you think you can control all of them?"

He grinned. "That's precisely the point. I can't control all of them. I really don't want to. You see, these creatures—in their present numbers, anyway—represent a change in my plans. Usulkan was to be my headquarters world, a power base from which—ah, but the Federation changed that. So now I too have changed, not the overall plan, but some of the elements. On some ten worlds where we as Hunters have plied our trade, my friend, I have organizations ready to topple the existing governments. None are Federation worlds, but such a pattern would not be overlooked by them, *could* not be overlooked by them, in that once they suspected that the same organization was responsible for such far-flung events they would see that organization as a very real threat to the Federation itself. And such will be the case, I assure you—although that's a long-term consideration. But suspicion can be lessened after the coups, if I have time to do some extensive clean-up work. That's what the Naumum will buy me—time."

I didn't quite follow his logic and said so.

"Usulkan is now a Federation planet. The event which at first checked me now is turned to my advantage. The Federation must protect its own, correct? Without the demonstrated ability that it can do so, there is no advantage for any world to accept membership in a regime that offers little else in the way of benefits but much in the way of oppression. Therefore, when my little grand-children's crates are shattered near the shorelines of Usul-kan—"

He stopped abruptly, seeing that I'd got the picture. It was not a very nice picture, being one of complete havoc. All shipping, above and below the water, would be destroyed. But that was just the beginning of it. The Naumum would not stop their killing at the water's edge. Though they preferred the deep waters, if they were pro-grammed correctly . . . and I had no doubt that they were programmed correctly. The Federation would have to put all the muscle available into the fight—for appear-ance's sake, if nothing else—and that would buy him plenty of time. But within that time—

Two thousand of them!

The business end of the blaster gestured ominously. "Any move toward those air-controls would be your last, my friend. Although this way might be as good a way to die as the one I have in mind. Gentlemen."

Two more blasters appeared in the doorway.

"Outfit my friend here with a suitable breathing ap-paratus. Bring him to the Number Three lock when he is ready." He returned his attention to the vu-thru cages, then he turned back to me.

"All of my grandchildren are not exactly alike. Would you care to select the individual with whom you're to do battle?"

"I wouldn't want you to accuse me of rigging the match," I said with a lightness I did not at all feel.

CHAPTER 13

"Generous," I commented as the smiling Ku-Sidor extended the dart pistol to me. It wasn't loaded and wouldn't be until I located the clip awaiting me between the two locks leading to the outside. In addition to the gun, I was returned my steel knife. That was to be it. A dart pistol and a knife. The odds were lousy, and not increased much by the fact that the helmet I was given featured a mounted red lamp. That gave me the use of my sight in just one direction, whichever way the lamp was pointed. The Naumum's three eyes would need no assist of that kind.

Fourteen was waiting at the inner lock.

"Looks harmless, doesn't he?" he said, hefting the small cage. "But then, as we Hunters well know, looks do deceive. I do hope you'll put up as good a scrap as you can. We'll all be watching on view-screen and we haven't had much sport down here."

"I'll do my best," I said through my teeth.

"Excellent."

He nodded, and the inner lock was opened. It closed behind me as I found the clip of darts in the passageway. I swore. Normally the clip carried six darts. There were but three allowed me. One for each eye. I swore again.

"Don't dawdle in there." The voice over the speaker was unusually cheery. But there wasn't much reason for me to hang around. Some things are best got over quickly.

I opened the second lock and stepped inside. As I sealed it, the air bubble rose from below and moved me upward to the final hatch. It opened automatically, and now I was surrounded by the dark waters of the deep. Waters into which shortly would be injected something small and just as dark. Small at first, that is.

I touched the top of the lamp and its beam lit up the side of the hatch. Then, pistol in right hand and knife in left, I waited. I had no plan of battle. What battle plan would be of much use? The thought crossed my mind that I might try to outrun the beast, but I dismissed it. The Naumum could outswim me easily, and he'd have the advantage of coming at me with my back turned. Besides, there was one small advantage I'd have staying close in by the structures on the sea floor—that of maneuverability. He'd have just a little difficulty in moving in and around the series of hatches and terminals as he chased—

Chased.

Defensive thinking, Hunter!

Damned right it is. And don't give me that crap about the best defense being an offense. What in blazes do I have to offend *with*?

Three darts and a sharp blade. At least, I hoped it was sharp. For that matter, I hoped the damned pistol was in working order. I was not about to waste one third of my ammunition testing.

Besides, I didn't have the time. The air bubbles coming from a lock off to the right told me that in no uncertain terms. As did what was in the middle of all those bubbles.

I'd never seen a Naumum grow. Even considering the circumstances, it was a fantastic sight. First there was nothing—or if the eye could catch anything it was no more than a tiny fist-sized inkblot of black against the slightly lighter blackness of the surrounding water. Then, as if you had your eye trained on it with the aid of a high-powered zoom lens which suddenly zoomed in, *whammo!* A full-grown Naumum.

It was like a vid commercial for some food product. Simply add water and serve. Instant killer.

Instant killer in search of a victim, that is. Maybe, if I got in close to him while he was still adjusting to his surroundings. . .

It seemed like a good idea. Anyway, it was the only idea which came to me right then. There were some thirty yards separating us, thirty yards of empty sea, except for one piece of hardware on the sea bottom. A search-light terminal with tubelight pointing directly upward. Not much help visually since the light was out. Not much in the way of a protective structure, but maybe the speed of attack would compensate me for what otherwise might be a stupid move. After all, the newborn would have to adapt to his new size as well as his new surroundings. That might easily take the fifty seconds it would take me to get into a position for a good shot.

In actual fact, it took him about twenty-five. Not that I was counting, mind you. I had just reached a point over the searchlight, which was halfway between the two hatches, when with three rapid eyeblinks and a wriggle of all four legs the baby-faced nemesis charged. I take back the baby-face reference. The glinting reflection from my red lamp showed me rows of five fully developed adult-size fangs.

I shot downward to the searchlight, wondering just how much protection I could expect from it. Not much, I figured, since the device was not much taller than an average man and only about four feet in diameter. Nonetheless, that was all there was available—if in fact I could make it.

I did, with a good five seconds' grace period, which I put to use in aiming my pistol carefully—straight at the cornea of the Naumum's middle eye. There was a spot just under the lower jaw that would have served me better. The trouble was, that spot wasn't exposed. Anyway, I had two extra darts to play with. That is, if the pistol fired.

Cheer up, Hunter. Then you'd have *three* extra darts.

He was no farther than six feet from me, the spotlight housing between us, when I pulled the trigger. The weapon fired, the dart dropping in directly where I'd intended it to. As the Naumum's four appendages reached up into the writhing jaws and above them in shuddering spasms, I watched for a suitable opening through the fury to his throat. Suddenly I heard myself laughing, but then I realized it wasn't me, although it was my voice. Thoughtfully, Fourteen had provided my mask with a communicator.

"Excellent shot, my friend. But those darts of yours aren't really long enough to do any real damage. I'm afraid they'll serve only to irritate your big opponent."

Irritated he was, all right. As he dropped his arm-legs, the two good eyes he had were looking for blood.

I took aim again. As I did, Fourteen made it plain he was trying to upset me:

"By the way, you may not know that the Naumum can navigate fully in the blackest of waters. He'll be able to find you, even if you take out all three of his eyes."

I squeezed the trigger carefully, and the creature again writhed in pain.

"One eye to go and we'll find out," I said into the speaker.

"*Bravo!*" Fourteen returned.

I shouldn't have taken the time out for idle conversation. One of the Naumum's thick legs whipped out and cracked into my right shoulder which in turn drove my left shoulder into the spotlight housing. In time—but just barely—I saw a second of the creature's bludgeons creeping around the other way. I buried my third dart in the sensitive feeler tip, which reflexively jumped back.

My third and last dart. And him with still one good eye to see—

To see.

I had just enough seconds to borrow a trick which a clever but now deceased Ku-Sidor had pulled on me earlier. Except that I'd have to be a bit more convincing if I wasn't going to end up in the same now-deceased state.

There were three motions, but I performed the first two as one. One, rip off red light and push it out to my right. Two, spring upward to the face of the searchlight. Then three, kick-off from that footing directly at that third eye, the steel knife-point serving as head to my human arrow. Once the decision to act was made there was no turning back. Fortunate it was, then, that the ruse worked. The operative eye was focused on the light which two of the beast's arms crushed between it. My light and his eye became inoperative in the same instant.

The knife sank deep—too deep. Because my right hand was too forward on the rear of the blade, it too sank into the newly carved cavity in the softness ahead of it. Hand and knife came out together with a sucking sound just as the frenzied arm that shot up caught me under the chest and sent me flailing backward to crack once more into the searchlight housing.

But this time the crack was more than just a figure of speech. The entire top half of the housing—including the lens and lamp—snapped free and joined me in what now was a swirl of mud on the sea floor. I struggled to get to my feet, trying to free myself from the tangle of the wires and cable that were wrapped around me like the tentacles I knew would be coming in a matter of seconds. Now my movements were as frenzied as the Naumum's had been. It was as if I were caught in the grips of some gigantic deadly snake—

Or eel!

With a quick series of kicks I rose straight up in the water, shedding the smaller wires, but keeping the larger and heavier cable with me—at first not by choice, but then as it began to uncoil and sink of its own weight I wrapped both hands around the slippery plastic insulation, letting go of my knife to do so. It was a risky business, this, especially since I wasn't sure I could hold the thick cable for much longer.

But I saw immediately that I wouldn't have to. Fourteen was right. What the Naumum couldn't see, he sould smell—or something. Whatever the exact nature of his sensory perception, he had located me and, as Fourteen also had said, he looked irritated. That was a clear case of understatement. The Naumum was in a rage.

He was coming fast. On my part, I was moving as fast as I could—backing off, and when the beast had risen to a point horizontal to me, down. Now, if I only timed this right, if when those viselike jaws of his opened—

Now!

Reversing my direction I pushed toward the five rows of teeth—pushed with my feet and pushed with my aching hands. Then I snapped back—just as those teeth clamped savagely together, the electrical cable between them.

The sea water lit up like a New Year's celebration. How many volts were going through cable and Naumum I had no idea, but the number was adequate—not only to fry the creature who now would not and could not rid himself of his man-made killer eel but to send a charge through myself which almost charred my brain. We dropped through the still sparkling water together. The difference was that I was able to navigate under my own power—but just a little.

Fourteen was both unhappy and happy. Not at the same time, but in one-two order. Unhappily, he said, "Damn you—you've got my killer with trickery!" Then came the happy part: "Fortunately—or unfortunately for you—someone else is just as angry as I am."

I tried to clear my vision, but realized that the sparks I saw now were from within. Outside of my head, the real sparks suddenly disappeared. Something was between me and them. It was, of course, the someone else to whom Fourteen had referred.

And quite conceivably, Grandfather Naumum might be angry with me.

It was as good a time as any to take the easy way. Immediately I blanked out.

How long I was out I can't vouch for, but it was clear that I'd been moved a great distance from where I'd started. As my eyes accustomed themselves to the light, I realized that there shouldn't be any light where I was— unless I'd not been moved very far and this strange place with the rock walls really was inside the complex somehow. But no. I remembered being moved. Dragged. And this light—it was from an assortment of headlamps, all grouped on the floor of this enclosure, just as if it were aboveground and someone had a fire going of logs.

"I have increased your air supply from among the tanks I have collected."

I turned from where I had been looking. With one of his tentacles, Grandfather Naumum extended a long object to me.

"This is but one of the dart weapons I have amassed here. It is also all right for us to converse. I changed the frequency of your communicator. They—the ones inside the great dome—think you are dead, and it would not be useful to let them know different."

"Why is it I'm not dead?" Not that I was complaining, mind you. It seemed to be the appropriate question to ask. "After all, I killed one of your—"

"One of my species. I have some questions to ask you, then I shall tell you what is in my mind. First question, which I do not understand, is this. You are the bossman here, yet you are not the bossman, otherwise you would not have been placed outside to be killed. It was not an accident, I know that because the little Naumum could not have been released by accident. Or is it that your own kind turned against you in a revolt?"

For a first question, that covered a bit of ground. I did the best I could, explaining first that I was not the top man in the outfit, but that I'd come to investigate what was going on here.

"Namely, because these people have been using the facilities of my company to build their structure. Their leader also has been using my face."

The Naumum corrected me. "More than that. He is the same body. I mean, it is two bodies, your and his, but they are the same. What I mean is—"

"I understand what you mean. But have I answered your question."

"First one, yes. Even though I do not fully comprehend, but that is not important. The workings of man-brains and Naumum-brains are different. Second question now: Do you know what it is they are doing here and why is it they have brought me and the other Naumums here?"

"They plan to turn all of them loose in the sea. All of the Naumum."

Grandfather considered this. "There is much life on this world? Life-forms like yours?"

I nodded. "There'll be a hell of a lot less if those Naumum get free."

"Thus you would slay them first?"

The question came out in a level tone, with no indication of whether that was his suspicion or whether it simply was a question. I had a vision of having my limbs torn from my trunk, but I answered in the spirit which appeared to match his.

"I would, yes."

There was a pause that lasted at least three human life-spans. Then:

"Yes, you are right. I will help you slay them."

I exhaled half the oxygen in the tank.

The Naumum continued, "Yes, I will help. They—the men inside—they have done something to the brains of the little ones. I do not know what it is, but they did not do it to me. I can remember only being in the tanks for a little. The thoughts of hate and killing were everywhere in my brain, but then they took me out and told me that I would act as sentry for them. I have done so for a long time now, it seems. The little one I saw this day was the only other they released. I could sense what emotions he gave off. Naumum are not killers, but they had made this one a killer, a ravager. It is my thought that they have made all the Naumum such. Is this truth?"

"It is. If they were let loose they would attempt to kill every form of animal life—on sea or land—that this planet has.'

"Then it is a must that they be destroyed."

"That's easier to say than it will be to do."

"You? You are not afraid, that I know. Why do you say it will not be easy?"

I laughed. "We are one Naumum and one man."

"And you are one man who has the explosive power. You destroyed a large ship."

"Sure, but what happens if I tried to explode the dome that way? I'd be releasing thousands of your kind into the seawater."

Another pause.

"You are right. I did not think of that. Therefore we shall have to destroy them in another way. Wait—"

If the Naumum had an ear visible I would say that he cocked it then. After a couple of seconds in which he held that strange pose, he scrambled from me and from the range of the lights. I just about had time to wonder where he had gone off to, when he was back.

"All right," he said. "Continue what you were saying."

"I wasn't saying. You were—about how we could destroy—"

"Yes. The air. If the master control could be turned off, we destroy both human and Naumum inside."

"Excellent. Where is the master control?"

"You do not know?"

"No." What's more, it wouldn't have made much difference if I did. Something as important as the master air control would have built-in fail-safes from here to Sunday. But the air control regulating the mixture going into the Naumum room—that might be another matter. That we might be able to take out.

We? Of the two of us, man and Naumum, only the man had a chance to get that close. I said as much to Grandpa.

"Perhaps, but I will go in with you as far as I can. A Naumum is not easy to kill."

"So I've found. Now, about weapons—for me, I mean. A dart rifle is all right, but have you got any with explosive warheads?"

He repeated my last two words. I explained what I meant, then he maneuvered a couple of the lamps to a corner in the cave. There was a healthy pile of weaponry.

"You can take whatever useful is there."

I began rooting through the rifles and various types of pistols. "How did you happen to come by this stuff?"

"Now and then, men would come that for one reason or another the headman did not want to leave alive. Then too sometimes men from the inside became ill and died. I, as I have said, am sentry. I also am to keep the area surrounding the dome clean of the dead. The dead I deposited elsewhere. Their implements here. I thought the artifacts might come to be of use someday."

I hoped he was right. Unfortunately, the pile of arms contained no warheaded darts. Nor was there a blaster, which I had hopes of finding. The heaviest weapon on scene was a stunner which, on high power, might—

I chose two dart pistols and the stunner, placing all of them in my suitbelt. Crisscrossing two bandoliers of darts over my shoulders, I nodded to the Naumum.

"Those are enough?"

I told him about the plastic around the exterior of my boot and how it worked. He seemed doubtful.

"You just place it somewhere and it blows up fifteen minutes after? How long is fifteen minutes?"

"From the time you went out to capture that girl to the time the ship exploded.'

He did not comment, but appeared to absorb this information. Then he dipped two of his tentacles into the pile of red lamps and extended two to me. He had seen and, no doubt, had approved of my earlier stratagem, but seeing them both in his tentacles gave me another idea.

"We'll need seven," I said.

"Seven?"

"I'll carry three, you four. When we switch them all on—if we have to—we'll look like a larger force."

"Speaking of which, we had better hurry."

"Speaking of which?"

"Yes. When I went outside a bit ago it was to listen better. There is a sizable force—small vessels but fast—coming closer to our position. They might not be friendly to us, but even if they are not they might do the wrong thing. Such as—"

"Such as try to blow the dome to smithereens," I completed. Satu, if in fact it was him—and if it wasn't I'd kick his butt—would have no way of knowing.

"Smithereens?" the Naumum asked.

"Never mind. Let's move." As he turned to lead the way, I noticed something I didn't like. It was instinct, but nonetheless—

"You've got five lamps there."

"So?"

"You were supposed to carry four, me three. For a total of seven."

"And seven is a magical number?"

"You're damned right it is."

As he dropped the extra lamp with what I interpreted as a shoulderless shrug, I thought to myself, *It had better be.*

CHAPTER 14

"There's one other consideration," I said as we came out of the rock enclosure. "The girl—the one you dutifully captured and brought inside. She's a good friend of mine. I'd like to get her out alive."

"You, human, may attempt this if that is your wish. But do not ask me to consider it of importance. She is but one single thing of your race. I am to see thousands of mine perish, if we have success."

It was a point against which there was no effective argument. There never was, that was the trouble with war. When so many were to die, what was one single life? Regardless of the meaning you as an individual might attach to it, it was without meaning. Just a cipher, a digit, one stroke on the score-pad, if in fact you were keeping that kind of tally. One down, more to go. A Hunter should know better. This Hunter did know better. But that didn't make the pending reality easy. Could I find Jana? Could I get her out? Those are the kinds of questions asked by

heroes in stupid romantic fiction. In real life, friend—
shed all the tears you want about it—there was never
enough time. If, accidentally and without eating up the
ever-ticking clock too much, I could get Jana of the firm
thighs out of this mess, I would give it a try. Otherwise . . .

Well, it had been nice while it lasted.

End of subject, consideration—and maybe of Jana.
So goes the war. And the war itself didn't look all that
good, either.

The cave to which the Naumum had taken me was
quite a ways off from the dome. First element: time. How
long it would take us to cross the distance I didn't know.
At least, there was a bit of good news connected with that
time element.

"They're slowing down," Grandfather said. "Almost
to a treadwater."

"Good," I replied. It was. In the first place it was a
good indication that the approaching vessels were my
own men. A group of ships friendly to the dome would
have advance-communicated their approach. Only somebody with less than friendly intentions would slow to a
crawl. The second good thing about the slowdown was
the longer it would take them to reach target. We'd get
there first, Naumum said.

"There is the matter of the sensors," he added. "They
still are ahead of us, and I can get through them easily.
But the ships which follow . . ."

"Can we take out the sensors without setting off an
alarm inside?" I asked.

"No, and I do not think you would want to do that.
When the alarms sound, they will have to respond."

I saw his point. My men would offer a diversion, while
I did my work. That fact alone the Naumum saw. The
companion fact that a good many bones might rot in the
seaweed he didn't see, or if he did it didn't bother him
much. As with Jana, so with Satu and the others. Maybe,
though, if we moved fast enough—

But I was disabused of that notion fast.

"I hope we can get inside before the alarm goes," he said. "It will be close, but it would be much better for you to be past the chamber section before the men inside have to use it to reach their vessels."

"Wait." I stopped my swimming and came to rest on the bottom. "How far apart are those sensors?"

"Much distance—the first ones. They get closer as we get closer."

I thought for a moment. It might work, depending upon Grandfather's replies to my questions.

"Can you communicate to those inside the dome?"

"Yes, if my transmitter is activated."

Good so far. Second: "Will they allow you to come inside the hatch without suspicion?"

"If there is a good reason, yes."

Very good. Now, the real kicker: "Could you smuggle me inside—under your body—without my presence showing up on any sensors?"

Now it was his turn to think. "If . . . if you had no mechanical thing that would register . . . the headlamp pack, for instance . . ."

"Never mind the headlamps. I've got a good use for them—all seven of them." I told him what I had in mind. He seemed pleased.

"Now I know that human brains work different than mine. Better sometimes. I would not have thought—"

"Let's just get it done."

We worked rapidly. Naumum knew the direction from which my ships were coming. It was comparatively easy to place the headlamps in position. Spaced properly, they formed a single-pronged arrow, which any pilot would recognize as a sign to proceed in a single file formation— slowly. If they followed the direction, they would easily get through the first two bands of sensors. There were five in all, the Grandfather said. By the time my fleet hit the last two, reaction time inside would be severely limited.

Hopefully, I myself would be creating a bit of diversion within their midst. Anyway, it was at the third band we had to accomplish the tricky part.

Or the Naumum did. It was a double-edged act. Destroy and explain.

The destroy part was easy. A macelike swat of one tentacle took the sensor out in a cloud of mud and metal parts.

The explain part depended upon Grandfather's prowess as an actor. Once his communicator was on, he did pretty well.

"Hello, inside. I think I broke something out here," he said.

"What happened?" came a furious voice from the receiver.

"I just wasn't watching where I was going. Was it something important? Can I help to fix it?"

Fury turned to disgust. "No, never mind. We'll get one of the maintenance boys on it. How about that man we sent out earlier? Did you take care of him?"

"I took very good care of him," the Naumum answered, and signed off.

As he did so, I saw I had nothing to worry about—not as far as his being an actor. His three eyes closed and opened rapidly in what obviously was a tripartite wink.

We were between the last two warning rings when we sighted the red lamp of the maintenance man pass up far to our right. Though I now had no lamp of my own, my faceplate was designed to pick it up clearly and it did. It would not have, had not a space opened up between the Naumum's front and rear tentacles. I was tightly grasping his rear left unit which, to do the creature credit, he tried to move as little as possible. Still and all, it was turning out to be a bone-jarring trip into the dome. In that we were maintaining communicator silence now that the Grandfather was booked in on the dome master channel,

I couldn't even complain about the new bruises I felt building up on what already was a body with more than its share of old ones.

The pattern was as direct and fast as the Naumum dared make it without causing any undue suspicion on the inside. He waited until we were nearing one of the larger intake hatches before he spoke. In the blackness I could see nothing, not even the hatch, let alone the dome which had to lay just yards beyond it.

"Hello, inside. I found something. I think you ought to see it. Should I bring it in?"

"What is it you've found?"

"I don't know, but it looks strange. Do you want me to bring it in?"

There was an exchange of voices out of radio pickup range. Then:

"What does it look like? Can you describe it?"

"Naumum terms of description are not human terms. In your terms, no, I cannot describe it."

Another out-of-range exchange.

"Look, I can see by sensor control which hatch you're at. Move you and your big find over toward the nearest vid camera. That way we all can get a good look at it."

"Vid camera?" the Naumum repeated dumbly. "I do not know this vid camera. Maybe you just want to forget what I found. OK?"

"*No!*"

A third exchange which this time sounded like a two-sided swearing contest.

"OK. You bring it in with you. Someone will meet you down at the inner lock."

The hatch cover slowly began to open outward. Gripping me tightly—a little *too* tightly—with his tentacle and swinging me up to the topmost part of his head, the Naumum slipped up and over into the hatch. It was a smart move on his part. This way he would be visible first, and also could drop me in a way that his bulky form would be between me and whatever eyes there would be to otherwise see the two loaded and cocked dart pistols I gripped in my two eager hands.

As water was replaced by the enveloping bubble of air, there was only one thing worrying me. No, check that. There were lots of things bothering me, but one specific immediate problem. As I knew from experience, there were vid cameras in the entry tube between the outer and inner locks. If the Naumum was *not* lying when he said he knew nothing of these contraptions, he wouldn't know enough to make sure his form was placed in a position to block out eyes which might be pondering the interior screens.

By luck or the Naumum's design, we got past the point where I was sure there must have been a camera trained on the outer lock. Unfortunately, the boys upstairs were even more clever. The sound box came alive.

"Naumum—lay the thing you've found on the floor. Then step back and we shall be able to see it. Naumum —what are you *doing?*"

I was wondering the same thing, except that I had a little better appreciation of the speed involved in whatever it was the Naumum was doing. The crashing impact gave me my answer. As he whisked me around his body, I saw that a Naumum-sized fist had collided with the door of the inner lock. The door had given way nicely.

"Thanks," I said. There seemed little reason for secrecy now. There was only reason for speed. I therefore was a bit surprised by the retaining grasp of my leg. It was only momentary, but as the Grandfather's tentacle pulled back, I saw he had enough exposed plastic in his possession to create a brand-new under-sea canyon.

"Fifteen minutes, human," he said. Then he thrust me through the passageway he'd created.

"*Crush him!*" came the order over the voice box I slammed against the wall of the corridor opposite the yawning steel and began running around to my left. A sound behind me told me that the gap had been sealed and another sound—one of screaming metal—told me further that the *him* which was to be crushed was not myself—not yet, anyway. They had depressurized the tube between the two locks. Depending upon the gauge of metal used, and upon the composition of Naumum exterior hide, behind me right now was one of two things. Either a heap of scrap metal or a mushy Naumum. Speaking of which—

The blaster shot that careened off the wall high to my left would have turned me into a very similar mush. The firer, however, had got his shot off too soon, before he had me clearly in his sights. I did the same thing, but was luckier—also I let him have a dart from each pistol. One of them, I can't say which, caught him neatly in the forehead.

The man behind him got his first in the ear. The second slammed into his heart.

There was no man behind him. Not yet. I took time to pause and make the first man's blaster my own, leaving behind the dart pistol my right hand had carried. So it wasn't exactly a fair trade—he didn't complain.

All right. Now that I had an effective weapon, what was I supposed to do with it? What were my real chances of getting to the Naumum room?

And where exactly was that from here?

I stopped running. I did so in order to try to get my bearings, but instantly was glad. Not that I had a flash of insight as to which part of the complex I was in—other than the fact I was in the farthest corridor from the center of the dome, something I knew as I had entered it. No, that wasn't it. What *was* it were the footfalls I heard thudding toward me. Several of them—and from both directions.

I figured I had a good twenty seconds. Good? There was nothing good about it. I now took a close look at this section of corridor in which I found myself trapped.

To my left was the outer wall of the dome. To the right, the curving wall contained a number of doors, each containing a seal-wheel. Moving to the closest one, I turned the wheel. It clicked open. I moved forward to the next, and turned that wheel. It did *not* click open. As the feet-to-floor sounds pounded louder in my ears, I made my decision—without benefit of eenie-meenie-miney-moe's. I blasted a huge gaping hole in the locked door and kicked it open. The man inside was another of those bastard Suryans. I took off the right side of his face. Then I backed down the corridor to the unlocked door.

And entered.

I closed the door quietly just as the sound of clacking thunder halted up the hall. The sound of the voices was muffled but the excitement was fully evident. And now more thunder from the opposite direction, then a halt called. New voices in the chorus. Fine. I had to see where this room led to.

I checked the wall closest to the other room first, and exhaled with relief to see there was no adjoining door. If there had been, right there and then when I was congratulating myself for a ruse well done, the best laid plans of mice and men would have blown up in my face.

The room was lighted dimly by an overhead phosphorescent lamp. It was bare of all furniture and furnishings. Completely empty. There was but one way out—other than the one from which I'd entered, and raw wisdom dictated that was the last exit to choose, even in the case of extreme emergency.

As it happened, it was a case of extreme emergency.

At least, the giant of a man with the sonic pistol in his fist looked that way. Especially since that same sonic pistol was pointed somewhere directly between my nostrils, and my friendly weapons were aimed at a neutral slab of metal flooring.

He was a large black Rim Worlder, not that it mattered.

What mattered at the moment was his weapon—and the funny look on his face. A sort of confusion—

Of course.

"You!" I snapped. "What are you doing in here? Aren't you aware that an enemy is loose inside the dome?"

The confusion spread. "But, sir—I was told to stay here and guard—"

"Don't be stupid. And would you kindly redirect that pistol?"

As he followed that last order, he began what probably was to be a string of profuse apologies. Confusion had turned to acceptance of authority which, in turn, changed back to confusion again as he tried to comprehend the sudden gaping hole in his chest. With his last gasp I think he comprehended that my pistol too had been redirected, then fired. In any case, he made a valiant try to get me in his sights again before he crashed face-first to the floor.

I stepped over him and entered the room he'd come from. This room, like the others I'd been in so far, had the typical overhead lighting. What was not typical was its furnishings. It was a sparsely furnished apartment, its features including a washbasin, a chair, and a narrow cot.

The girl on the cot wriggled her greeting as best as her bonds allowed her.

I tried to be gentle as I stripped the adhesive from over her mouth. Then I went to work on the wire that held her wrists together.

"Kal, what's going on here? Who are these people?"

"Rub some circulation into your wrists. I'll get your ankles loose."

"Kal, please—don't ignore my questions."

I turned on her so fast her entire frame seemed to shrink in upon itself.

"Listen, my sweet. I left you twice today, and twice you chose to disobey me. All right. What's done is done. You're here and there's nothing much I can do about it except get you out—or *try* to get you out. You may have overstepped yourself this time."

Her tearducts looked as if they weren't going to be able to stand the strain. We Hunters have our moments of sympathy, I guess.

"You took out Trow real professionally, I gather. What did you use?"

Salt water creased into the ends of her smile. "Extended knuckle blow—roundhouse to just over the ear."

"Of course, his back was turned to you at the time—"

"What do you expect? A formal invitation to observe?"

I laughed. So did she; then: "Kal, please—can't you tell me—"

"No. You don't have time to hear it." I took my watch from my wrist and fastened it to hers. Then I told her where she was in relation to the recently blown exit.

"You wait for ten minutes—ten. No more, no less. Then you get yourself out of this dome just as fast as you can—and as far from it as you can. There will be some ships outside. Satu is in one of them. He'll take care of you. Here, you'll need this—and maybe these."

The *this* was my airpack and mask. The *these* were my blaster, dart pistol, and the two bandoliers of darts. With all that weaponry, she might be mistaken for one of the insiders. I hoped she wouldn't find herself in a position where she might have to use any of it. On her part, when she again was standing and fully garbed with all my dubious gifts, she seemed to be most concerned over the airpack unit.

"What about you, Kal? How do you get out?"

I gripped her shoulders hard. "Maybe I don't. If not, remember me fondly. Ten minutes, Jana. Then run. You understand?"

She nodded.

There was a door on the wall adjacent to the one I'd used to enter. Obviously it led to something deeper into the interior of the dome, but what? I asked Jana.

"I don't know, all these corridors and rooms look alike to me."

Not unnatural. But, all right, there was no other way for me to go. I went back to the body of the Rim Worlder and hefted his sonic gun, then I stepped past Jana to the interior door. She reached out for me with her hand, then stopped the movement.

"Kal—"

"Good luck, Jana."

There might have been more I wanted to say. There might have been more I wanted to do. But the timing was far from right for either.

CHAPTER 15

There were two advantages I carried with me as the president of Sub-Oceanic. One was my familiarity with how under-sea installations were laid out. The second was my familiarity with the types of devices which normally formed important parts of these facilities. The fact that company equipment and planning had been used in the design of this one was what made both of these areas of knowledge advantageous. It was handy to know, for example, that the blue-painted corridor in which I found myself would lead eventually to an intersection which would be red in color and would cut inward directly to the central control area. From the diagram of this structure, I knew that there were five of these red passageways in all, all radiating outward from central as the beams of some lonely sun. It was also handy to know that, spotted randomly throughout the walls of red, would be a number of sound beams which served not only as alarm signals but which also served as very effective man-stoppers.

These was a third advantage I carried with me in addition to the two just mentioned. My face.

The guard at the blue-red intersection snapped to attention, then sagged to the floor as the life went out of him. There were no other guards in sight, which was fortunate—because for the moment my hands were free of weapons. Hoisting the dead guard up over my right shoulder, I pressed the side of my face to the left wall, peering down its length. There it was—on the far side of a panel door—the little black slit in the wall-facing that betrayed the presence of the sound beam. Or at least there was one of them. I crossed to the right wall and repeated the sighting process. It was fortunate I did. The tiny slit in that wall surface was only five yards from where I stood.

Now came the gamble. Keeping my eyes trained on the deadly little black slit, I carried my corpse burden to a spot three feet from it. Standing him up on his own two feet, I shoved him through the beam. The slit in the wall was level to the man's shoulder as he passed it, but the setting was such that the beam caught him just above the hips.

There was the sound of searing heat. And the disgusting smell of heat-seared flesh. The guard hit the floor beyond in what was almost two pieces.

Somewhere farther in the interior of the dome an alarm was sounding and lights were flashing. I could hear or see none of this, but I knew it was happening. The one thing I didn't know was how the sound-beam units were activated. There were two possibilities. In normal circumstances, one unit's going into action would immediately cut off the entire system in that corridor. This was for several reasons, among which was the possibility of accidental tripping. The fail-safe device would allow others to get into the corridor to assist the injured—if there was anything left to assist. Also, in the case of attack, the cutting out of a corridor upon the sound signal would allow the interior forces to move in for battle.

However, there was the other possible setting which automatically did nothing—which, in other words, left everything as it was. I had gambled on the situation being otherwise. If I had won, I had a free run to the end of the red corridor—before they could get a complete vid-scan on screen. Aiming my pistol at the point where the guard had been hit, I squeezed off a shot. Sound beam met sound beam in a mirror nova that staggered me backward three full steps.

I'd gambled and lost.

Now from the blue corridor came the sound of boots meeting metal. Several boots. My way of retreat being closed—

The white spot of sound-beam-contact still burning in my eyes, I moved two feet from it, crouched low, and with all the power my legs could muster, executed the highest dive I could. My landing was less than graceful, but I'd made it past the beam—with all my parts. Now, if only that panel door between me and the next beam wasn't locked.

It wasn't. It slid open just as the shout was raised from behind me. Even before my eyes rested on the four riflemen in the blue-and-red intersection, my sonic gun was firing. Wildly, to be sure, but I figured that if I sprayed my shots wild enough—

A series of sustained sound-to-sound suns flashed between us. As I continued to create more of the energy blasts, I stripped a small—very small—bit of plastic from my boot-top. A time bomb it might be, but like any time bomb, if it were hit with a sudden blast of sound—

My pitch was underhanded and careful—but I missed

the wall unit. No big problem, although you like to do things right. I trained my own sound weapon on the plastic strip, then dived head-first into the open room.

The blast shifted my landing place from floor to wall. Maybe I should have used less plastic.

Shaking my brain free from its whirling dervish images, I scanned the room I had entered. There was no other exit—even though a sharp-edged hole had been torn in the wall nearest the blast, it wasn't large enough for a man to squeeze through. Or so I thought.

The Suryan dwarf with the large pistol got both head and pistol through easily.

"You're dead if you move," he said nastily.

"Obey him, Hunter," said the voice box over my head. I could see the tiny camera lens to the side of it as well. "Drop your weapon, please. You've given us an excellent run. The least I can do is buy you a drink. Brandy, as usual?"

The vid-screens in the central control room were dead, but it was by choice, the switches being off. Fourteen raised his brandy snifter a little higher than was customary. I followed his eyes upward toward the top of the dome. The small needle-nosed vessel at the top of the steel slat-ladder looked ready to go. I gathered from Fourteen's comment that such was the case.

"Each of them—my men—think they are part of a special cadre which I'll take with me when I depart. It's a very convenient vessel, however, easy for one man to operate."

"You're running?"

He shrugged. "I have little choice. The dome is surrounded."

"Good man, Satu," I said.

"I suppose. But, then, all of us connected with Hunters Associated are good men, are we not? I suppose you're wondering why I've allowed you to live till now?"

"Out of respect for my resourcefulness, no doubt."

Fourteen laughed. "I'll give you your claim to fame on that score, my look-alike. In the game which is called survival you've managed to do very nicely. But, no, the real reason you're alive is that I have a use for you. But I'll get to that in a moment."

"You don't have a chance," I said. "Those ships out there will tear you apart."

"They'll possibly tear the dome apart, yes. But do you really think they'll be able to withstand an attack of some two thousand Naumum?"

"No. But then you'd be shooting your entire wad, right?"

"Correct, but I may as well. As I told you, Usulkan is no longer of any use to me—especially now. There is no reason why my diversionary operation should not begin at once. Things are fairly well on key at my primary locations, and I am getting a bit anxious."

"Look, maybe we can make a deal." It sounded frail, because it was. But I had no idea how little strength I was leading from. Not until a man on one of the control boards called to Fourteen that he'd picked up something on sensor.

"Second fleet of ships—coming in fast. Also commander of first fleet insists on talking to you."

Second fleet?

Fourteen grinned. "This *is* turning out to be interesting. And here I thought you were bluffing about our friend Satu being out there. You see, that first fleet— it isn't yours. It definitely isn't."

He depressed a switch. A vid-screen jumped into life. The face on communicator-camera definitely wasn't Satu's.

"Go ahead, Captain," Fourteen said. "We have been able to restore some semblance of communication."

"Restore, crap! You listen and you listen real good. You now have five minutes—five—to evacuate that dome. Otherwise we destroy it. Do you understand me?"

"I understand you perfectly, Captain. I'm sorry, but I'm afraid the communicator is weakening again. I'll try to have it repaired shortly."

"Five—"

The screen was turned off, as was the voice. Fourteen's grin was wider now as he turned to me.

I had no grin at all. Although I hadn't recognized the captain's face, I had indeed recognized the emblem he wore on his tunic—the four multicolored planets in concentric orbits.

There wasn't a man on Usulkan—or most places—who wouldn't recognize the insignia of the Federation.

"Very clever, the Federation. They traced our last importation vessel straight here. So, as should be obvious to you, the game at this end is played out. Very clever of them. But they also are very generous. You heard him —he gave me five full minutes. In exactly three minutes, I shall give the order for my men to go out after the Federation ships, to attack them."

"They won't stand a chance. Another diversion?"

"Not at all, friend Hunter, not at all. You see, each of them will be bringing with them a little vu-thru box. You know the type."

"Your pals must be big on suicide."

"They are, they are. As long as their bossman is with them, leading the way. Do you get the idea?"

I did. There was now no doubt in my mind as to why I was still alive. "What makes you think I'll cooperate? What makes you think I won't make you kill me right here and now?"

"The lovely Jana makes me think that," he said. "If you cooperate, she stay alive. She goes with me—if you're a good boy."

"Jana's expendable," I said.

"We'll see. But I hope not. I really like the girl—but I'm sure you know how I must feel about her. Anyway, you have my word that if you don't cooperate the lovely lady will be food for a Naumum. Nasty way to go."

"Your word. That's worth a lot."

"Perhaps, but it's all you've got, brother."

The man at the control board had a new piece of intelligence. "The second fleet is trying to raise us, sir. On Sub-Oceanic wavelength. Any response?"

"Hell, no—wait." The thought going through his mind was one which seemed to amuse him. Then: "Yes, when I give you the word, punch in. I want them to receive my vid as well as audio."

He wrung his hands in expression of pure joy. "A golden opportunity, this. You know, I guess we share one thing in common, my friend. Though we're on the opposite sides right now, I would say that we equally hate the guts of our old fat pal Thumb. Watch closely, Hunter, as one of his own is about to bring down his little empire around his ears. Move back—out of vid-range."

The blaster in his hand meant business.

"First I talk to our little yellow man, then I exchange a word with the captain. By the time I'm done, Sub-Oceanic and Hunters Associated both will have their covers blown. Nice? Punch me in!"

I could see the vid-screen only from a poor angle, but I recognized the company's number two man.

"Satu—approach quickly and destroy those surrounding me. They're sporting phony Federation markings. Do you read me?"

Satu's voice came back clearly. "We're seven minutes away. Will that be time enough?"

"We clock you at less than three—hit them hard!"

He clicked off. The puzzled look on his face cleared when he saw my semi-smile.

"Ah. Seven minutes. Of course. A request for acknowledgment. Like you said—a good man, Satu. Nonetheless—"

He waved his hand, and the screen again became alive. This time I could see the Federation uniform.

"Captain—I have something to tell you," Fourteen began.

At which point I lunged.

He was fast, I give him that. The side-swing of his blaster caught me on the side of the head. But he made one small miscalculation. He had reacted involuntarily to what he thought was an attack upon his person. It was only after my left foot crashed through the vid-screen that he realized the truth.

"Get up!" His face now wore a fury that I thought I'd never see. As I looked up the barrel of the blaster he had trained on me I wondered how he could control himself not to squeeze the trigger. It was, of course, part of the thinking with which a Hunter was born into the organization. Anger is inefficient, went the maxim, and the corollary went: inefficiency is deadly.

"All right—*Seven*. This round goes to you. But the next is mine." He turned to the control board man. "Give the word. Everybody to the Naumum tanks."

CHAPTER 16

Time. How long had it been since the Grandfather had taken that wad of plastic from me? How long had it been since I'd left my watch with Jana? How long is fifteen minutes? The Grandfather had asked me that, and at the time I had thought it to be merely a question resulting from unfamiliarity with the units by which humans measure the passage of whatever stuff real time is composed. I had answered him in terms of two events and the distance between them, and that had clarified the problem. But what was the temporal distance between my being shoved through that inner hatch and this later instant as I walked at gunpoint from the control room to the place where the tiny Naumum waited? How long is fifteen minutes—or ten? Can the passage of time be clocked by the number of physical and emotional events which take place within it? Perhaps, if you're a Grandfather Naumum who has been accustomed to think in that way. But, if you're a human, a simple act—like that of diving over a sound beam in a red-painted corridor—can take from an instant to an eternity. Logic tells you the instant is closer to being more correct, and thus it should be measured accordingly. Fine, if that was the only event similar to it which took place, but it hadn't been—and the human mind, at least *this* human mind, was at bay. The plain unassailable fact was that some time had passed, and deep down it *felt* like I didn't have all that much to spare. There was another unassailable fact, as Fourteen called us to a halt.

We were at the Naumum room. I was where I'd wanted to be.

The problem was, so were about thirty of Fourteen's men.

None of them looked overly happy. It would have added to their edginess if they could have seen my face. But my air mask was tightly in place. Otherwise we looked exactly alike, Fourteen having taken pains to match-set our airpacks as well as to tear pieces out of his wet-suit corresponding to those I'd earned in a more legitimate if not more strenuous way. Still, however, some of the men obviously were wondering what a prisoner was doing inside the dome still alive. He explained it for them.

"We're giving them back their man," he said. "I'll take care of that just before—"

I needed no wristwatch or body clock to tell me the time I had been waiting for had come. The entire dome rocked with the impact.

A voice box screeched on: "Water in number five intake valve!"

An alarm bell rang furiously. Some distance away, men were screaming. A rush of water could be heard, soft, then getting slightly louder.

The eyes around me suddenly were staring wildly, all except Fourteen's. But even his weapon wavered for an instant.

The opportunity might be the last I'd have. Suddenly, between myself and my look-alike was a startled Ku-Sidor I'd yanked into place. Then, just as suddenly he was released, his arms flailing for support as Fourteen's blaster cut him down. But by that time, I'd knife-handed another of the men and had relieved him of his pistol— a dart gun.

"Get him!" Fourteen shouted.

As they moved to obey, the rush of water crashed dramatically higher in pitch and a small tidal wave rolled from the nearest corridor.

The screams now came from all around me. Instantly I was the forgotten target, the corridor farthest from the entering water now being considered the safe ground. And now between myself and Fourteen were several men, all pushing and gouging their way.

And then I saw that I had another problem. The voice-locked door to the Naumum vault was open!

But Fourteen was nowhere in sight. I knew where he'd be heading, but first—

I crashed through the arms and legs in my way and flung myself into the vault. The water-level was now over the sill, a wave of it causing me to lose my footing and slide into the central tanks. The controls! But which ones—

The hell with which ones! Dropping the dart gun I filled my hands with as many of the tubes as I could and yanked hard. The hissing sound which came out of the tube ends were like music to my ears. The water now lapping at my calves made a sound that was far from music. I grasped a second handful and pulled. Again the tubes broke free.

One of the cases to my left suddenly crashed open. The Naumum was about the size of a human head.

Crash followed crash as I spun back toward the door and shouldered through the opening. When the door was locked from the outside, I could hear nothing from within.

Lord—how many of them hadn't I killed? Regardless of how many, the vault couldn't hold them for very long. Anyway, it was beyond my handling now—no air cut-off would be effective now that there was water inside the tank.

But there was something I *could* do—one score I *could* settle. If I had the time, that is.

I grabbed a dart rifle which had been floating in the water, now up to my knees. Running, slipping, falling, half swimming, pulling myself around corners, I fought now with every ounce of energy I had in me. He had a head start, but not all that much that a dart couldn't span—not if I hurried.

Frightened men passed splashing through the corridors, all wild-eyed and with no thought of bothering with me, unless just a quick reflection that some stupid clod was going the wrong way. The roar of rushing water now was on all sides and building to a mountainous crescendo that I knew would bring this place down on everybody's ears in a very short time. But I knew—as well as Fourteen knew, we both being Kalian Pendek, builder of such installations—that the safest place was up at the dome top, the place where the escape ship was ready and waiting. I just hoped it still was waiting.

The control room, set slightly higher than the rest of the complex, had less than a foot of water on its floor as I sloshed into its interior. At the control board a man was slumped over the communication panels. It might have been the same operator I'd seen there earlier, but it was hard to tell. The top of his head was gone. Evidently, Fourteen hadn't wanted to take the time to explain where he was off to. Speaking of whom—

The console top to my left exploded in a rain of plasteel fragments. I dived behind the dead man, shouldering into his chair, and toppling him over into the water. I also heard the voice of the Federation captain.

"You haven't got a chance!"

Probably, I thought to myself. Then I saw what I was looking for.

He was only a quarter of the way up, crouched behind a metal support connecting his landing with the ladder. He knew—as I did—that he couldn't try another move, not in all that open space above. He'd have to take care of me first.

I turned back to the communicator.

"Captain—can you hear me?"

"Barely. Listen to me—"

"No, *you* listen. This is Kalian Pendek. You know the name?"

"I know it, but—"

"Just listen. The fleet behind yours is mine; the commander's name is Satu."

"We've been in contact. He has explained that you are inside, but—"

"Fine." At least Sub-Oceanic hadn't tried to take on the Federation mob. "Captain, how heavy are your vessels? About the same as mine?" I thought I knew the answer. The Grandfather had said the ships were small.

"About the same, but why—"

Another part of the console exploded. The Federation voice was no more. But I still had two messages to deliver.

"Captain, there's a woman out there—at least, I hope there is. She's probably wearing a couple of dart bandoliers. Try to find her. Then get the hell out of here—you and my ships, too. What's going to be coming out of this dome any time now is something you can't handle!"

Lecture over, I dropped to my face in the water. Whether my final words got through or not, I didn't know, but Fourteen's next blast took out the chance for any additional message.

Now I could concentrate on the last part of the job.

"Seven, you haven't got a prayer!" he called from his perch.

"So I've heard, very recently," I shouted back. "How do you figure your own chances?"

From somewhere outside the control room, a screeching of ripping metal added an audible question mark to my words.

"Don't be stupid, Seven. The two of us can make it. I can use a smart partner—especially one with your physical assets. With two of us, we can do twice as much!"

I had been swim-crawling between the rows of control consoles. As I reached a place where there was a space between two of them in the line to my front, I could see him clearly. He still was looking down to the communicator area where I had been. I had a front-side view that offered the best target I was going to get. I snapped up the dart rifle and fired.

Nothing happened.

Nothing, that is, except I'd given my position away—a position that now was itself a perfect target.

I managed to gut-slide a good five yards from that position before Fourteen's blaster turned it into raining confetti. There was another screech of yielding metal, this one closer. I was crawling fast now, trying to reach the far wall before—

But Fourteen had stopped firing. Of course. He'd have to stop if he was—

I cautiously lifted my head. Then I abandoned caution as I leaped over the counter top and straight-lined it for the bottom of the ladder. Both of Fourteen's hands now were busy going from rung to rung, his blaster tucked securely in his belt. He was now about a third of the way up.

I started climbing.

Like Fourteen, I used the sturdier metal ladder which was the main highway to the dome top. Right to its side, however, there was an auxiliary ladder made of a strong hemp. Originally it had served in the early construction days of the dome, but it was customary to leave these units in place as they made handy lifts for materials or tools needed at the top. Normally, I would not have given the rope unit a thought, but even in my furious scramble up its metal counterpart there were two considerations that made its presence of possible utility. The first was that, at any time, Fourteen could decide to pause for a moment and blast the bottom part of the metal ladder to splinters. That would make the free-swinging hemp version a life-saver, if only temporarily.

The second consideration came from my observing that, at a point just below where both ladders were attached to the topmost landing, the rope unit was tangled in the rungs of its metal sister. Highly optimistic thinking on my part, maybe, but if one of his feet hit one of those rungs in the right place and if at the same time I pulled hard outward on the hemp—

Really optimistic. Fourteen had decided to take that little pause. His aim was careful and directly upon his pursuer. I took to the rope and swung out hard. His first shot missed, but as his weapon swerved outward to intersect my swinging arc, I knew that his second—

But he didn't take a second. Even my attention was yanked from what appeared to be certain death to the crashing groan of metal from the dome walls below. A new tide of water rolled in, and with it, something else.

Two full-grown and murderous Naumum.

Six eyes scanned the interior, but not for long. As they fixed on the species they had been taught so well to hate, they charged toward the ladders.

For the moment, Fourteen forgot about the Hunter below. Now he took his second shot and his third and fourth. Continuing my climb on the steel unit now, I looked down only briefly to assess the damage. One of the Naumum lay half submerged in a mixture of water and his own blood. The other still came on—although with one less tentacle—straight for the base of the ladder. Did the creature think it could climb up these slats?

I passed the first landing, a third of the way up, before I knew what the Naumum had in mind. The platform began to shake violently. It was a simple expedient—the humans are on this puny piece of metal, therefore to rip it-from its place would bring the humans down. Fourteen, who now had less than a quarter of the way to go, evidently shared my deduction. We both transferred to the hemp unit at the same time, with not much time to spare.

The cracking sound was sharp and clear as, at the point where they joined the topmost platform, the rails of metal gave way. For an instant, the ladder paused as if deciding which way to topple. In the same instant, I planted both feet on the side of the now-free unit and pushed off. While not affecting the direction of the falling unit, the action served to swing the rope free as, with a sudden shudder, the heavy metal ladder swung inches past my hip, and, its top section slamming against the dome wall to my rear, split into some three or four pieces before crashing to the water below. Part of the unit had fallen squarely onto the Naumum's back. With baleful eyes and one free twitching tendril, he now recognized that he had been cheated of his prize.

"Now it's back to just you and me," Fourteen shouted. Without looking I knew I was back in blaster-sight again. But I looked, anyway, still attempting hand-over-hand to close the distance between us.

If you're going to get it, it might as well be by something you're looking at.

And I was sure enough looking at it. Fourteen, on his part, had waited for me to gaze up and into the muzzle of his weapon. The dramatic potential of the event had not been lost on him at all. His body looked relaxed as, his feet firmly planted on two of the hemp rungs, he held on to another with his left hand. His right hand, filled with blaster, was extended downward. His face was filled with an expression of triumph.

"Good-bye, Seven," he said levelly. He was no more than forty feet above me now, so I could almost see the minute movement of his finger behind the trigger-guard. There would follow the sight of a white-hot ball of light at the end of the barrel—and that would be final.

There was the sight of that ball of light.

But it wasn't final.

The hemp began a sudden jerking motion which almost tore Fourteen free from his perch. That relaxed confident posture almost cost him his life, right there and then. What it did cost him, in his wild attempt to secure a grip on the ladder, was his blaster. I grinned as I watched it fall past me. Following it down to water-level, I stopped grinning.

The rope hadn't stopped jerking. It wouldn't unless the Naumum whose lone usable tentacle was wrapped in its bottom portion either died from his earlier wounds or was successful in bringing this second ladder down from its high moorings. Survival again was the name of the game.

And the game was further compounded as, with an accompanying fragmentation of wall and floor, a new supply of exterior water roared into the dome area.

Fourteen's pause to kill had cost him about ten of the

feet which had been between us. His grapple to save himself from falling had cost him another five. So it was that as his hands grasped the underpinnings of the final platform, I was twenty-five feet below him. As he jerked his body up and over onto the landing, I thought I knew what would be coming next.

Unfortunately, I was right.

From the back of his belt it came, the glint of steel unmistakable. A simple blade, but effective enough when all it was asked to do was to cut through a couple of thick strands of hemp—especially when it was whip-sawing under a good thousand pounds of pressure from below.

As blade went into hemp, Fourteen said something down to me, but I couldn't hear it. The roar from below was too loud now.

It sounded like the palm of a hand slapping a face. Just as Fourteen's knife had severed one of the two strands, one of the moorings of the platform itself had torn free from the dome wall. As it did so, his weight on the edge of the landing caused it to dip suddenly downward. In his crouched position, he was off-balance to begin with. Then, too, there was the water-soaked and therefore slippery bottoms of his soles. In addition, there was my hand which now was tightly gripping his ankle—gripping and pulling!

The blade flew from his hand as his body arced out and over and down to grasp the hemp ladder which now whipped furiously on its single tenuous anchor. As I transferred my hands to the platform understructure and pulled myself over onto the platform, I could see that the frayed rope had not much time left to it.

"*Seven!*"

He was but five feet below the platform, his face that of a wild man.

"Help me, Seven! I'll tell you—how you can find out. About yourself! Who you *really* are!"

The platform was straining against the two bolts which remained to hold it in place. The escape ship was less than ten good strides from me. There was no time to waste.. Any instant now those other bolts could snap—or the entire creaking dome could collapse. I shouldn't have, but—

"How?" I yelled down at him.

"After we get to the ship!"

"No deal. *Now!"*

His head bobbed furiously in agreement. "All you have to do—"

Two things happened then. One of the remaining bolts snapped, and the strand of hemp ripped from its mooring. Fourteen held on to the very end, although I didn't wait to see his final splash. I had a ship to get to.

Only one bolt remained as I grasped the hatch-handle of the vessel. The superstructure holding the craft was intact, but there was a minor problem. The hatch was locked. Naturally. It was a ship only to be used for escape—one man's escape. And that one man had taken the secret of the lock's combination with him. Unless—

Regardless of individual differences, Hunters for the most part think alike. Then too there was a matter of precedence. The Naumum tank—

Pressing my face next to the lock, I hoped I'd be heard over the roaring crashes surrounding me.

"Fourteen," I said, as calmly as I could.

All too calmly, the hatch swung open.

CHAPTER 17

"You were most fortunate, Mr. Pendek."

The Federation commander's name was Stevvens. His morning presence in my office was not overly welcome, but he had his job to do. Besides, I should have felt grateful to the Feds—they did, after all, pull Jana out of the drink. She was resting at her apartments now. I wanted most to be resting in mine but, as the commander had said, there were a few things that needed clarification. And I was the only one who could do the clarifying. At least, I had been given the chance to shower and bandage a couple of wounds, and the commander was not the stuffy type who declined Satu's offer of a doubly strong martini.

"Most fortunate," he repeated. "The vessel you used to escape just cleared the dome before everything fell to pieces."

"I'm just thankful you didn't blast the ship to pieces," I replied.

"We were busy with other things at the time. Those ... what is their name?"

"Naumum."

"Yes. Scores of them. Most of them we didn't try to

engage. Your advice was excellent in that regard. We will, of course, initiate a hunt with bigger craft. I'm certain we'll get all of them."

I doubted it. The younger ones, maybe, but not wily Grandfather. He had made it out of the lock, that much was for certain. The first explosion had come from another area, Satu had reported. When I had time, I would pay a visit to a certain underwater cave I knew. There the future of the old Naumum would have to be decided.

"At first, you know, we thought you were responsible for the smuggling, Mr. Pendek. Your opposition to Usulkan's joining the Federation was well known to us."

I frowned. "I'm a businessman, Commander, a successful one. Frankly, Federation rule imposes a few regulations I'd rather not have to bother with, but that's the extent of my concern. You run your ships, I run mine. I think we can get by without much friction."

The commander hoped so. He had other points needing clarification. He also had some questions. Point: The dome and all its subsidiary facilities were built with Sub-Oceanic materials.

Clarification: Which was how I got wise to it—when my computer turned up the project, one that was unknown to myself and my managerial staff.

Point: Some sloppy management control there.

Clarification: Damned sloppy. Some corporate heads would roll as a result.

Point: The prefecture bureaucrats who posted the topside guards—they claim it was you yourself who arranged for this service.

Clarification: Our man was pretty clever, as the whole project shows. His cleverness included impersonating Kalian Pendek.

Question: He was a double?

Clarification: Good enough to pass a cursory inspection.

Question: But who was he—really?

Clarification: Your guess is as good as mine. If you find out, I'd like to be among the first to know.

Question: And his real aim—what was that? Why did he want to flood the seas with these Naumum?

Clarification: Maybe he didn't like the Federation much, either.

The commander rose. "Well, that about does it for now. I appreciate you'd like to get some rest, Mr. Pendek. If something more does occur to you, I trust you'll let us know."

I told him his trust was appropriate, and as Satu showed him to the door, I headed for the one to my apartments. One more little conversation and then I'd get that rest the commander appreciated I needed.

Thumb was spilling out of what I'd always regarded as being an ample-sized lounge chair. He clicked off the intercom with the office as I entered.

"Smart lads, those Federation people," he commented.

"Fourteen wasn't so dumb himself," I said.

"Not as smart as the master computer which finally alerted us. There were a few inconsistencies. Sorry that we could not have tipped you off sooner, but then you acted very well, Seven. Highly commendable." He paused, then stabbed a fleshy forefinger at me.

"I assume you have some questions, as usual."

"None," I said.

"None?"

"None that you'd answer. Sure, I'd like to know how Fourteen uncovered his true identity. I almost got that out of him, myself. Unfortunately—"

"Fortunately. And I speak in reference to yourself."

Another pause.

"I suppose you realize that we're going to have to scrap the Kalian Pendek identity. This recent business, when added to the consideration of Federation encroachment . . . well, the decision has been made."

"When and how?"

A wave of his thick hand. "Oh, two or three months from now. I'll leave the exact arrangements to your own discretion. In the interim, you'll have the chance to liquidate a sizable portion of Sub-Oceanic's assets. I'll be in contact soon as to where they should be transferred."

"And after liquidation of Kalian Pendek?"

"Back to Juang Luar as Jonothon Evvers. The identity will remain open for that purpose."

He heaved himself out of my chair. "And now you'll want to rest. I shall leave Usulkan this afternoon. There's a bit of mop-up to do on those worlds where Fourteen has been playing his revolution game. Not too difficult to handle, but it should have my personal attention. So if there's nothing further . . ."

He knew there was.

I started with the easiest. "There's Satu."

"A good loyal employee. He will be placed, and no doubt you will be meeting again on some other world."

"And Jana."

"Ah yes, the lovely Jana. How very fortunate that she did not have the opportunity to see you and Fourteen together. Otherwise . . . ah, but such was not the case. I suppose she will truly grieve after Kalian Pendek's demise, but that cannot be helped. In the meantime, Seven, enjoy. After all, you only live once."

Moments later as I lowered my back to the welcome touch of cool sheets, I thought about Thumb's last words. They were not exactly correct. Kalian Pendek already had died twice—very unpleasantly both times. But, yes, he would enjoy himself in the days and nights he had before death came again—the third and final time.

☐ **THE BOOK OF BRIAN ALDISS** by Brian W. Aldiss. A new and wonderful collection of his latest science fiction and fantasy masterpieces. (#UQ1029—95¢)

☐ **THE BOOK OF PHILIP K. DICK** by Philip K. Dick. A new treasury of the author's most unusual science fiction. (#UQ1044—95¢)

☐ **THE BOOK OF FRANK HERBERT** by Frank Herbert. Ten mind-tingling tales by the author of DUNE. (#UQ1039—95¢)

☐ **THE BOOK OF VAN VOGT** by A. E. van Vogt. A brand new collection of original and never-before anthologized novelettes and tales by this leading SF writer. (#UQ1004—95¢)

☐ **THE BOOK OF PHILIP JOSÉ FARMER** by Philip José Farmer. A selection of the author's best in all branches of science fiction, including the facts about Lord Greystoke and Kilgore Trout! (#UQ1063—95¢)

☐ **THE BOOK OF FRITZ LEIBER** by Fritz Leiber. Twenty pieces that cover all of Leiber's literary terrain. (#UQ1091—95¢)

DAW BOOKS are represented by the publishers of Signet and Mentor Books, THE NEW AMERICAN LIBRARY, INC.

THE NEW AMERICAN LIBRARY, INC.,
P.O. Box 999, Bergenfield, New Jersey 07621

Please send me the DAW BOOKS I have checked above. I am enclosing
$_____ (check or money order—no currency or C.O.D.'s).
Please include the list price plus 25¢ a copy to cover mailing costs.

Name_____

Address_____

City_____ State_____ Zip Code_____
Please allow at least 3 weeks for delivery